Takes A Pay Cut

NICHOLAS MITCHELL

Copyright © 2024 Nicholas Mitchell

Cover art by Erin Hoffert

All rights reserved.

No part of this publication may be reproduced, stored in a retrieval system, or transmitted, in any form, or by any means, electrical, mechanical, photocopying, recording, or otherwise without the prior written permission of the publisher or a license permitting restricted copying.

ISBN: 9798320933740

CONTENTS

Chapter 1	Pg1
Chapter 2	Pg15
Chapter 3	Pg19
Chapter 4	Pg22
Chapter 5	Pg29
Chapter 6	Pg40
Chapter 7	Pg48
Chapter 8	Pg53
Chapter 9	Pg55
Chapter 10	Pg58
Chapter 11	Pg62
Chapter 12	Pg67
Chapter 13	Pg70
Chapter 14	Pg73
Chapter 15	Pg76
Chapter 16	Pg83
Chapter 17	Pg87
Chapter 18	Pg90

CHAPTER 1

It was an amazing day for Death. Below the little city of New Wattsonville, and the rest of the world, The Underworld flourished. Reaping was far behind the reaper as world populations rose. A billion became three and five and eight billion by the Fall of 2019, although seasons had no bearing on Hell. Day after day, magma churned beneath red rock paved over by streets, by which demons and ghouls and foul creatures of the night traveled to day jobs or karaoke.

Cities had been made; what else was Death to do? He had resigned to his office desk to wade through paperwork as the working class handled the greater influx of souls. Gold coin was impractical, as newly founded banks digitized currency. Death had stolen the idea of a digital wallet from the heavens' department of human technology. The Man Upstairs wasn't pleased, although he never was pleased with Death.

Education had come before the cities. An economy

was only a dream without those qualified to run it. The souls of teachers and professors and specialists taught the unholy, and they taught their children until construction began. The people continued to praise Death for his leadership.

He disagreed. It flattered him, but boredom and necessity drove him. People drowned trying to swim in the lakes of fire, so he made boats. His secretary, Lucille, advised him to make boat guards in case of emergencies. It wasn't enough. His advisors asked him to enforce boating licenses, but those required courses and further development of government. Death couldn't be bothered to hire trustees so he delegated all law to his skeletal horse, Drake.

That same day, Lucille walked behind his desk while he was absent. She edited all of the documents relating to the Department of Transportation, giving herself all related responsibilities. The next week, after talking to Drake who didn't have much to add but a neigh and whinny, Death learned of this. He noticed that the horse was no longer wearing his "official government person" medal made from foil and gold marker found rolling in his dresser drawer. Death put in a formal request to the heavens for the appointment of an assistant god. The Big Guy, in all of his divine powers, granted him Charon. The matter was settled, albeit through complication.

Charon would be the only deity formally appointed as an assistant god. Various devils and entities filled the shoes of other mythical figures. Beelzebub was head of HR at the Duat, Hel was Cerberus' trainer and groomer, and so on. Lucille's younger sister, Lacey, was the Afterlife Accommodations Head. She ensured every soul's processing was to their liking. Death often found her in Elysium, a deserted place. The Greek afterlife was only perceived as mythology now.

"I've never been a fan of Elysium myself," Death said to her. She looked up, her blue skin against a white dress patterned in diamond shapes. Her blood-red hair was curlier than Lucille's and she preferred contacts. "It's pretty," Death continued. "But it's only trees and the occasional colosseum."

Lacey asked why he was there, and why he was talking about Elysium.

"Your sister sent me, saying something about a gala."

She said the gala wasn't over yet, then asked him why Lucille sent for her. "Why are you two planes of existence away from it then? Did they kick you out?"

The Seraphim guarding the heavenly gates had denied her entry. It was a divine gala, not an immortal gala.

"I'm sorry, but there's not much I can do about that." He sat down next to her on a fallen pillar of marble. The teal grasses swayed as he picked golden fruit from a vine. "I hate to agree with The Almighty, but that place is for gods only. That's not to say an imp can't be a god, but we're born godly," He bit into the fruit, but spat out the seeds. It was all seeds.

Lacey stood up, telling him she was ready to head back. Still sitting, Death looked up and said, "I hate that glorified lightbulb of a Lord anyways, so I'll tell you what: I'll host a gala of my own. Heck, I'll host fifty of them once I figure out what a gala is." She told him that it was likely what he had imagined a gala to be.

"Great, fifty fancy dress parties."

Thus, a gala was held every week for a year within the 9th Circle. It raised overall morale and productivity enough that Death added Galday to the seven, now eight-day calendar of The Underworld. One Galday in the Winter of 2020, Death had been busy twirling a rose drink around for the past hour when Lucille walked in.

She took it from him, reminding him that he had no digestive tract. Frankly, he didn't have much. It was as though a rotting corpse dumped in tar had its ears, nose, and lips cut off. His teeth shone white and a cyclopean eye covered the whole of his face. Those who didn't know him were frightened by his constant gaze. Death didn't smile, he didn't frown nor squint vertically, not that he could do any. He was forced to convey the majority of his expression in his tone of voice and body language.

"Why couldn't I?" Death asked Lucille.

"Mr. Reaper," she said. Her black skirt, white button-down, and thin-rimmed glasses gave her a sense of authority. Lucille's hair, as red as her sister's, was straight in a ponytail and her heels echoed on the black marble tiles. "I advise you to refrain from testing such."

"I don't have lungs, and there's nothing down there either. If I start drowning, just tip me upside down."

"With respect for your ideas, Mr. Reaper, I still don't recommend such."

"I've gone all these years without a drink or bite of anything, couldn't I have a teeny sip?"

"Fine, at your request," she held out the drink to him. He looked back for a few seconds.

"No, you're probably right. It's been so long since my tastebuds rotted anyway. Also my tongue, and my uvula,"

Galday was great for that first year or so, but the specialness of any gala faded with so many. Most of the damned and damning would stay at home or do anything else, leaving event halls empty of guests. People got used to the eighth day. Productivity lessened, but it was better than the seven-day calendar's yield. Lucille advised Death to remove Galday entirely, but he opted to rename the day Nalday and reduce Galas to once a year.

This was the nature of The Underworld. Death makes a new ruling, it sticks or it doesn't, and time goes on. There would always be things like healthcare or worker unions and luxury taxes, and there would always be paperwork on his desk. He wasn't one of those who complained about immortality, but he began to miss his reaping days.

One billion humans prior was the height of his career. Every day was spent trying to find a new way for someone to die. It had to be believable though; spontaneous combustion was often out of the question. A craft knife could fall from a starving artist's apartment and cut a hanging wire before said wire would swing down and electrocute a passerby. Death was himself and his art. Contrary to popular belief, it wasn't a lonely job either. He'd often talk to soldiers or patients or those about to die. Some would try to tell others they had seen him or talked to him, but nobody believed them. When his day was over, Death would return to The Underworld. Time there flowed differently, so he rarely missed any targets during a nap.

Complications only arose those years later at the desk. The Man Upstairs saw the development of The Underworld as a distraction. He couldn't argue with some demons' productivity, but the rest was unnecessary. His Holiness argued that Death himself should process the souls, not those born from the depths of evil. That, however, would mean more paperwork for Death. Anything was better than paperwork.

He had stood his ground, but Lucille pushed him to do more. He wouldn't; The Lord could vaporize Death for anything he wished. There was no good reason to poke that bear. For the time being, he would have to be content with the arrangement.

June 21, 2021, there was a knock at the door that echoed through the halls of his gothic cathedral mansion. Death had been lazing on his couch with a bag of cheese curls as Drake stared at the wall. He got up, stretched what muscles he had, and walked, and walked past pillars and statues of black marble, down the foyer steps that circled Lucille's desk, and up to the doors stretched far above him. He pushed them open to find a face engulfed in blue flame.

"I'm retired," he told them.

"I know," they said. Their voice sounded deep, but it rose in emphasis. "I'm not here for a favor." They wore a suit with black and white pinstripes and black leather shoes.

Death was still wearing his skull and crossbones pajamas so he shut the door, said a small incantation which turned the pajamas into a cloak, and opened it again. "Come in."

They walked the whole way back to Death's office. Death himself pulled two chairs up to the towering windows overlooking The Underworld. Deceit sat, watching him rummage through various desk drawers before finding two glasses and a vintage bottle of Tortured Tears. He walked back to the chairs with the glasses between his fingers, holding one out for Deceit. He poured Deceit and himself a glassful before setting the bottle on the ground and sat down with him.

"What kind of wine glows?" Deceit asked.

"It isn't wine. Some of the souls processed secrete this stuff and ghouls like to bottle it. Zero calories and zero alcoholic content, but it evaporates in the stomach."

"Freaky," Deceit took a sip, but the drink burned up. The rim of the glass melted as well. He saw Death take a sip and exhale a mist of wailing faces.

"So, what is it this time? A fatal misunderstanding, some backstabbing, poisoning of some kind?"

"I told you, I'm not here for a favor. I'm just checking up on you."

"For what? The job's been the same for the past while. The Underworld's running smoothly despite

The Big Guy's disliking. What's going on up there?"

"The major gods are still doing their thing, Junction and Connectivity got married, and other minor gods are still disgruntled. Same old, same old."

"Is that it?"

"Yeah, and I'm surprised you're fine with that."

"There's nothing you or I can do about our jobs, that's that. I'm fine down here, look," Death tipped his glass towards the window. Endless miles of city stretched outwards, soul processing facilities hung from the cavernous ceiling of The Underworld. "I made all of that; I can make everything I need."

"As infinite as it all is, The Underworld is nothing but red rock and hot stuff. You have enough of your demons working to process the souls, why not ask The Almighty to let you work on Earth again?"

"I'd rather quit altogether before asking him for something. There's only so much talk of purity and greatness that I can take."

"Well, he's The God, creator of all and the one truth. I don't mean to sound preachy, but that whole spiel isn't wrong."

"Yeah, a self-absorbed bastardization of a truth," Death stood from his chair and walked to the couch, grabbing his cheese curls.

"I know he sucks," Deceit called. "But talking to him couldn't hurt."

In between crunches of curl and cheese, Death said, "It could hurt a lot! 'Divine beam of holy lasers' kind of a lot!"

"Well, maybe. I don't think he could kill Death though."

"I'm sure he will find a way. In the meantime, do you want to watch Ghoul's Anatomy? It's the start of the new season."

"I have work to do."

"The patient is a pishacha."

"Really?"

"And the episode's only half an hour."

"Fine, but you should consider what I said."

Deceit sat down beside Death on the couch, sinking into a large, gray cushion. As he reached into the bag of cheese curls, he noticed how warm the cushion was. It was getting warmer. Behind him, the couch had caught blue fire from his head.

"Mr. Reaper, I have these permit requests, but," Lucille paused as she looked at them both, the couch engulfed in flame as credits were sliding across the television screen. "Why is the couch on fire."

"Hey, Lucy!" Deceit said. Lucille could see the silhouette of his hand waving through the flames. "You just missed this pishacha getting arrested for health care fraud."

"Sorry about the couch," Death said. "It's warm and cozy though."

Deceit stood up from the couch which, by then, had become a tall pile of ash, and walked up to Lucille. He put his arm on her shoulder and said, "He's not wrong, The Underworld is a great place, but I agree with you. If watching dramas is the most fun thing he can do, he needs his old job back."

Lucille nodded. He patted her shoulder twice before walking past, presumably to leave. A minute later, the blue flames vanished as a naked Death was left sitting in the ash like it was a beanbag. Fortunately, he had no organs or features to be embarrassed of, so he stood up and summoned a new cloak.

Once Lucille had swept the room and gathered her papers, she walked over to Death at his desk. "Mr. Reaper, he's not wrong, you could get your old job back."

"Or, The God could vaporize me. I don't think any of you realize how much he hates me."

"Why do you think he hates you?" She leaned over his shoulder with the question.

"I haven't been the best god, but I've seen some others that are way worse. Alcoholism was too drunk to keep alcoholics drunk!"

"Mr. Reaper, maybe he's hard on you because you're his most important god."

"I have never spoken once to the man. He refuses to talk to anyone in person because it's 'too great an honor for a being divine to converse with those below' him. It's always some Seraph or Archangel."

"Then try, at least try. There's no reason to give up if you've never asked him about job positions before."

"Talking to him could risk my people. If he acknowledges my job is too much for me alone, he might send his angels down to do it instead of my demons and creatures. Then, they'd be out of a job and The Underworld would return to barbarism and torture. I don't know why The Lord thought everyone down here was psyched to hurt people for eternity."

"But Mr. Reaper," Lucille tried to say.

"No. They're expendable to him, same as his angels. I'm not bringing any of that feudalist stuff here."

"Yes, Mr. Reaper. I wish I could help more."

"You're helping more than enough. Disregarding your secretarial work, just having you here keeps me sane."

"Thank you. However, you should try to work something out."

"You're dismissed, take the day off."

"Yes, Mr. Reaper."

  Lucille left Death his list of missed calls, left the office, and pulled the double doors closed with a gentle click. Her heels clicked on the foyer stairs and she came around to her desk. There was one landline phone, a pen, and a notepad before a bolted swivel chair. Instead of entering her room behind, she exited the mansion.

The air was crisp with sulfur. As she leaned on the

balcony rail high above the city of Asphel, she could hear the growl of the thermal plant above the lakes of fire; the flow of spirits clouded above her. It was too much. She liked The Underworld, but it shouldn't have needed any development. It was an oversight on The Lord's part, but also on the part of the minor gods. Help from a few of them, Management or Processing or the like, would have solved everything. The minutiae of every god's role drastically reduced workloads. The list of minor gods related to Fire was hundreds and Reaction was practically out of a job. The major gods got to relax, the minor gods weren't stressed, and Death governed hundreds of millions of souls and Underworldlings.

Lucille knew this– had always known this –and had always known the implications. She only received a hundred calls and a few dozen forms to fill a day, there were rarely any visitors, and Death wasn't surprised.

She stopped staring and grabbed her phone to call Lacey. Lucille asked if she was fine, if she had eaten yet, and how work was. Lacey worked in accounting and loathed it. She understood numbers and math and everything she wouldn't bore her sister with, but it was tedious. The day never seemed to wane for Lacey.

Lucille laughed a little and said that she would get along well with Death. She told Lacey to remember to eat lunch and to be careful in Asphel. They had lived there their whole lives, less than a decade on Earth but thirty in The Underworld. It was a safe place, as was everywhere developed, so they had always joked about getting stabbed or mugged. Guardians or deities of myth were always around, taking pride in their purpose of maintaining safety.

"Drake," Death said from his office chair. His hands were pressed together with deep thought. "What's up with the gods of rain and fertility?"

Drake stood there.

"My buddy Beelzebub used to be a deity of those a while back. Apparently, destruction and murder and flies weren't always his thing and he went by the name Hadad," He held up a photo of a portly, sleeping man with a bull-horned helmet rested on his stomach and marker drawn on his face. "It's a college photo, I couldn't find anything more flattering. Anyways, I was chatting with this really weird but handsome guy Dante who told me that this other dude, Tlāloc, took his place!"

Drake stood there.

"Dante said he wasn't a bad guy, but The Big Guy started complaining about too much rain and crowdedness and sent Hadad down here. Crazy stuff, I tell you. I don't know any of the heavens' policies, maybe there was a limit on archetypes, but even so…"

Drake clopped behind Death and stood by the far window.

Death regretted giving Lucille the day off, so when he left his mansion he was elated to see her. "Lucille!" He said. "I gave you the day off, what are you still doing here?"

Lucille turned towards him, surprised he wasn't at his desk. "That's my business, Mr. Reaper," She said. "Although I ought to ask you the same."

"I was looking through that stack of missed calls you gave me. Simply looking at it made me tired, so I tried talking to Drake instead. Drake wasn't getting me."

"Would you like me to make the calls for you?" She adjusted her glasses. They were straight already.

"Would you? I'm sorry, I didn't mean to pull a fast one on you."

"No worries, Mr. Reaper," she said with a smile.

Death had trusted her to speak on his behalf. So, as she went through the list, Death stamped reports. After some time, a few hundred soul reports had been confirmed and every missed call was answered. Each soul report accounted for a thousand souls, each processed and tallied by his government employees.

Lucille came to his desk once her calls were done. Death decided to call it a day. The next day, Death left to go fishing for the World Serpent while Lucille met Lacey at a coffee shop near Lacey's work. As Death looped a small hammer on his hook, blue flames flickered around him.

"You're still going for it?" Deceit asked. Death's boat rocked with his arrival.

"Nothing bad could happen," Death said. He was wearing a pale blue vest and a bucket hat. "Everything that's swimming here is a scrapped idea from The God, he can put them back if it's a problem."

"You want to risk a big snake crushing Earth?"

"Please, even I could handle it. I'm sure it hasn't eaten anything between all of these mouthfuls of lava."

"That's a lot of faith you're putting in lava."

"Isn't it magic lava or something? They're the great lakes of fire."

"Magic isn't real and a World Serpent isn't going to mind a little heat."

"This again?" Death turned, his fishing pole nearly smacking Deceit in the face. "If we're all gods and we can do whatever, why couldn't magic exist?"

"I'm sure it could, but The Almighty doesn't have a purpose for it; It can, but it just doesn't."

"Well, that's lame. Either way, I doubt it could kill me."

"I'd like to agree, but the only thing keeping you invincible is The Big Guy's blessing. Make sure to stay on his good side."

"Yeah, sure. Don't you have work to do? People to lie to?"

"Not down here I don't."

"Then get up there already!"

When Death turned his back to Deceit, the blue flames disappeared. He wouldn't be discouraged from fishing for the World Serpent. Even if he didn't catch it that day, or the next, or any day, he would try still.

"What's new with you?" Lacey asked Lucille. She was holding a two-bean roast with everything syrup.

Lucille was surprised that two ground beans constituted coffee for her sister. "Work is great, only a hundred and something calls today."

"Really? Don't you have a schedule to write or something?"

"Not today, Death gave me the rest of the day off after taking his calls."

"That's nothing! Doesn't His Darkness have great matters to attend to?"

"Probably, but he doesn't work that way."

"Why do you think so?" Lacey leaned over the table.

"He prefers automation; efficiency. If there's something someone can do for him, that's great. If there's something that can do it for that someone, even better. I'm sure he only hired me out of pity."

"Don't say that! You do a lot."

"Like?"

"Well, I don't have anything specific. You take care of me often."

"I'd call that a responsibility, not a job."

"But there's a lot that you can do. I'm sure you would do plenty if asked."

"That's true. How was today for you?"

"Horrible. So, remember when I was talking about Amy yesterday?" Lacey went on for some time about Amy, "Then, my cruller fell. There was only a bite left, but she started laughing for like, a minute straight," and so on. Lucille was spent by the time she got to the bottom of that roast, a sticky residue left at the bottom of Lacey's cup. Still, the two hugged as Lucille slipped her a small envelope. Lacey left the coffee shop. Lucille looked out the window and watched her walk down the road. She looked back at the booth, staring into her cold cup half empty. It stared back.

Lucille slipped and caught herself on a table. She slowly leaned towards the cup again to find a single eye staring through: Death's eye. "What was that about?" He asked Lucille.

"What was 'what' about? What the hell are you doing in my coffee?!"

"Jeez, my bad, I just didn't want to walk all the way there. I'm calling to ask about a report I received of physical currency, somehow, flowing into two bank accounts with your last name. I'm sorry to intrude, but I've never seen something so weird."

"It's nothing troubling, Mr. Reaper. I'm the receiver of our parents' inheritance, so I split it between Lacey and me each month."

"I see, my apologies. I thought the banks had taken care of every coin. Plus, I got a new Secretary of the Treasury."

"Ms. Janess is gone?"

"Yeah, she had a baby: a little Yōkai with wings."

"Send her my best regards."

"Will do. Oh, and about your money situation, don't worry about handling the coin. I'll get it all processed and tell the bank to start transferring the money to you both unless you want to collect interest in a savings account."

"That is very thoughtful of you Mr. Reaper! However, I would like to maintain the transfers as they are. Thank you for handling the rest."

"Anytime." Death's eye disappeared as Lucille leaned back. She began to notice the people around her staring at her and her cup. Lucille left the booth and the shop with haste.

CHAPTER 2

The arrival of The Lord's Seraphim in The Underworld rang in the New Year. It was time for Death's yearly statement for 2020. A heavenly gate appeared above Death's desk as angelic figures descended into his office. First came a pair of Seraphim whose heads were revolving discs of gold. Many eyes peered from the rings' metal. Then came a march of trumpeting Angels and guarding Archangels. Lastly, a mirror descended from the gate. Light poured from it and filled not Death's mansion, but the whole of The Underworld.

Death sat before the display, twirling his pen. The Angels had piqued his interest. They had plain faces and all sorts of hair. He could have been mistaken, yet he swore to himself he saw a name tag on one Angel. Lucille kneeled beside him. Death remained seated at his desk despite her tugging at his pant leg.

"As his holiness descends, you may all be honored," a Seraph said. "The Mightiest God shall speak."

"It is as they say," The God's voice came from the mirror. "You have been given the honor of my presence. You may proceed with the accountancy, wretched one."

Death sat up and leaned forward in his chair. He slid a stack of papers across the desk, towards The God. "You will find all records of the souls processed during the year 2020 here, my Greatness."

"Is that all? Have you not prepared to present me with such information?"

"Do you dishonor our Almighty?" One Archangel asked, their hands gripped on their sheathed swords. Lucille couldn't bear to look.

"I don't," Death said. "You will find this to be most concise. As I know your time is valuable, it is with urgency that I address another matter I believe to be pressing."

"Lord?" The Archangel asked The God.

"If it is as you say, I will allow such." The God said.

"Cool, cool," Death said. He set his pen down and stood from his chair. "Not too long ago, I spoke with one of my associates about my duties as Death. I was reluctant to agree, but after careful consideration, I believe that you owe me an apology."

The room was silent. Although Lucille had suggested talking to The Almighty about sorting his workload, she didn't mean to disrespect The God.

"An apology?" The God asked. "I am the purest of all beings, capable of nothing that would necessitate such. Must I correct you?"

"You have given me the honorable responsibility of processing all of Earth's souls," Death said with a bow. "However, I feel myself undeserving of such a divine offer as I pale in comparison to your might. I only ask that you allow me to divide the work further amongst my people, as they too are products of your divine creation."

"Are you suggesting that one of my creations, you who were molded by my hands, is incapable of fulfilling their purpose?"

"I can fulfill my purpose and exceed it, my Lord. Earth has simply outgrown my original purpose. Please, as you are so famously humble, I beg that you make amends with the people of Earth by giving The Underworld the grace of further employment."

The Angels started to stir. The Archangels drew their swords. The Seraphim weren't sure who they should look at, but then The God spoke. "You are correct, I am the purest and humblest of beings. I will grant this grace, only because your suggestion is the product of my own creation."

"Thank you, your holy, shining, great greatness. May your angels travel in safety to the heavens above."

The mirror, the angels, the archangels, and the seraphim left through the heavenly gate as it vanished into light. Death looked towards Lucille, her head still lowered.

"They're gone," He said. She didn't move. "They're gone-gone, the light faded."

Death heard an audible exhale from Lucille before she said, "We are extremely lucky to be alive." She looked up at him.

"I know how he works, asking for an apology is so insane that he can't fathom a god not asking for a good reason. It's that far beyond his imagination."

"Even so, you held all of The Underworld hostage in your negotiations."

"If it hadn't worked, I would have had more to say. It did work though. Our workforce is bolstered and I can work comfortably for the foreseeable eternity."

For some time, Death did work comfortably.

Every now and then he had a pet project or a corporate mess to fix himself, but things were fine. 2021 saw little change in The Underworld. The global death rate jumped in 2022 but the demon workforce enlisted Tsukumogami (possessed tools) to keep up with the extra paperwork. Strange souls without a cause of death appeared in 2023 to Death's bewilderment. In April of 2024, something impossible happened.

A large, red, and gray soul came into The Underworld. There had never been a soul that wasn't blue before. It shook and flickered and, despite its defiance, it felt fragile in the palm of one demon. Death was called down to the main soul processing facility. He appeared before the soul in an instant. There wasn't a fancy portal, or a flash of light, or any dark mist; he was simply there.

"Is there a name?" Death asked the closest demon.

"No," they said. "There isn't one that I can find. Born on December 9, 302 in what is now the Czech Republic, in an unnamed Germanic town, they disappeared shortly after birth. There isn't anything after that, but it says they lived to be 1720 years old. They died November 10, 2023."

"Are you sure? Did they tell you this themselves?"

"They did not, that is simply what their record says."

"Have they said anything at all?"

"Not a word."

As Death looked at the soul, it continued to weakly shake. He put his hand over it, around it, he even poked it some, but nothing different happened. Then, as he picked it up, his entire body ached. It would have been debilitating if Death was not used to the feeling.

CHAPTER 3

Back when Death reaped souls by hand, he often encountered minor gods. Some he had little to say to, such as Tripping and Clumsiness, but sometimes he would have a chat with gods like Loss or Risk. During a war on the Eastern side of Earth, one he was too busy during to even catch the name of, Death often crossed paths with Agony.

Due to all of the violence, they never had the chance to talk. Now and then, though, they would shake hands. Death discovered the immense pain that Agony inflicts by a single touch. As not to be rude, he continued to shake hands with Agony without a word.

It was because of this war that the influx of souls into The Underworld became too much to bear, resigning Death to his desk where he continued to work for years. The pain he felt shaking Agony's hand was the same pain he felt holding that discolored soul.

"This is Agony," Death said plainly. "The minor god. This is his soul."

"The record says it's a Germanic human soul," The demon said.

"That doesn't matter, this is Agony. Agony is dead."

Gods didn't die. Each god was a being The God created to assist him in maintaining Earth's order, blessed with eternal life and invulnerability. Yet, there was Agony's fading soul. Souls didn't fade either, every soul in The God's foreseen destiny was to be kept immortal in The Underworld. It seemed that the gods' souls weren't foreseen.

As Death clutched Agony, Agony's soul faded into nothing, the last wisps floating away. Despite whatever implications or consequences such a passing would have, Death could only look at the phones of his employees. Every worker had received an automatic email about a registered soul missing, the first ever to be sent.

No god would kill a god. Death wasn't even sure a god could be killed. This had to be a human's doing. If it were, it would only be more evidence of The God's mismanagement of Earth. No longer was his boss a pain to deal with, he had cost Earth a heavenly life.

Death reappeared in his office as Lucille walked up to him. She asked what had happened. He recounted what happened plainly.

"Is the death of Agony our responsibility?" Lucille asked. It was the first time she was asking Death what to do. She was at a loss for words.

"This isn't about managing souls anymore, Lucille. No matter what The God tells us to do next, the impossible has happened. It's unlikely he would answer questions if he knew how Agony died. I need to go to Earth to investigate."

"What? That isn't your job Mr. Reaper. If you're trying to use this as an excuse to reap souls yourself, such is unacceptable. You may have The Underworld handling the souls, but your duty remains here."

"It's not that. Agony had a soul. I don't know what that means; I don't know how he died. What does that mean for me? For The God? Does he have a soul?"

"Sir, you can't let your imagination go wild. We need you here and we need you focused, The God could arrive at any moment."

"I will talk to him, but not now. I need to figure out what could have happened first."

"The scale of Earth is far larger than you could imagine. You can't travel every corner and find evidence amongst ten billion humans! I respect you wholeheartedly, so please, don't do anything rash."

"I have to go, now, before The God arrives. He ruined my job, he almost ruined The Underworld, and now a god has died under his careful watch. I can't stand to work under him and under such conditions, not until this is solved."

"Sir!" Lucille begged.

Death walked to his desk and pulled a thin piece of chalk from a drawer. He walked back to the center of the room and started to draw various shapes and lines surrounding a circle. Soon, he had completed a ritual chalk circle. The God would find it harder to track Death through Witchcraft's God-Approved Emergency-Teleportation reserved for moving humans, stray souls, Underworldlings, and angelic beings. It wouldn't cover his tracks for long, The God is all-seeing.

"Goodbye Lucille, and good luck," Death said. He vanished in a white burst of light as the chalk on the ground burned up.

CHAPTER 4

After leaving The Underworld, Death awoke somewhere unfamiliar. Light beamed from a large hole above and he found himself covered in muck. He also felt a sharp pain on the back of his head and had trouble seeing much outside of the light. Soon, someone stuck their head through the hole. They were wearing some sort of yellow mask but didn't care to ask what he was doing. The person left. Drenched or not, Death had to figure out where he was. He never put coordinates into the chalk circle, evidence of it could have led The God to him sooner.

He began to recognize his surroundings as a sewer tunnel. If he were to leave, he would be seen by humans. Humans usually couldn't see Death, but he wasn't on Earth for official reasons. There couldn't be a chance that someone would see him.

Death started down one tunnel, weaving his way through the sewers. Now and then, he would check a manhole cover to see what was above. Whatever he was planning, he needed fresh clothes and a disguise once he emerged. Disguising his rotten skin, he climbed into an alleyway as a thirty-something short-haired brunet, the sort you'd see in an ad for wireless data at reasonable prices. Looking around the corner, he found a Scandinavian home store crammed between an abandoned Sears and a coffee shop. The abandoned Sears would have to do for fresh clothing.

Thankfully, no one around felt like bothering a cloaked man drenched in sewage prying boards off of a Sears entrance. Inside, most of the shelves were empty, but the lights were still on and there was still a storage room. The ceiling had a blue and green Sears logo spray painted on it, yellow eyes staring from the letters' curves and loops. Perhaps The Underworld needed spray paint too. A cardigan with jeans and casual loafers was the only fitting outfit left. With new clothes, a job would be next. He would probably need money for bribes or goods or whatever he couldn't account for. When it came to choosing a job, Death was a very skilled person. It was unfortunate that most of those skills held no relevancy on Earth. However, the Scandinavian home store looked like an easy place to work, moving boxes and filling shelves.

The application process was surprisingly easy. After lying about his email, education, phone number, address, and work experience without being asked for confirmation, Death was hired. He was put on the night shift to move boxes to warehouse shelves and organize displays. Although other employees loitered in the building after hours, still wearing their blue and yellow uniforms, Death was the only one on the night shift. He previously worked the graveyard shift, so it should have been easy enough.

His daytime coworkers were racing around on pallet jacks even though they could go home. Some were playing hide and seek, he even saw some playing house in the displays. It was childish but childlike wonder could have been the latest trend for all he knew, he hadn't been on Earth in so long. After filling half of his shelves, he visited the cafeteria. One of the cooks had also stayed, making themselves and some employees dinner. Did they all live here? It was only eleven at night though; Death last heard on Earth that many people stay up until morning when they don't have anything better to do. Lucille had told him a lot about humans, but he'd only directly spoken to patients or soldiers before.

Returning to his shift, Death noticed there were more employees than before. They were probably somewhere he hadn't been before and only just came out.

"So, pallet jacks?" Death said.

"Yes, I love racing." Said an employee.

"Yeah, that's cool. Could you spare one? I have a shipment of GRÖNKULLAs I need to move."

The employee silently smiled at him with bloodshot eyes. He kept waiting for a response, peeking past him at another jack race. There didn't appear to be a race track, rather, the other employees weaved around shelves. Suddenly, a spray can landed near his foot from somewhere above. Death picked it up and was about to ask whose it was but felt a tap on his shoulder.

"Man, almost hit you there. Sorry about that." The person speaking was wearing a maroon hoodie and a white mask painted with ink blots. "I thought I was the rat around here before I saw them."

"Excuse my asking, but who are you?" Death asked.

"Arouros, graffiti artist. You don't have a problem with me being here, do you? They don't seem to mind."

"I guess not? You're not stealing anything, right?"

"No, no, I just like having somewhere my work can't be washed away." He pointed towards a mural on the ceiling depicting stacks of boxes labeled fragile. Eyes peeked between each box. "Oh, my manners man, who're you?"

"Deaauhm, uh, Damien. Sorry, sore throat."

"Haven't met a Damien before. Well, good luck dealing with those wackos. You should visit the cafeteria when you can, a guy named Matt cooks everything and it's properly good. He's the only person I've met here with two cents to give other than you."

"I'll make sure to stop by there, thanks." Death watched as Arouros climbed back up the shelves, passing out of view. The GRÖNKULLAs were his only company now. They were soft enough as bed sheets, but the mattresses were rigid. The bed frames didn't help either; each plank was held by two wooden pegs ready to snap.

Once finished, Death went to the cafeteria. As the night wore on, employees left, letting him hear the echo of his footsteps against the thin stairs. Staring in between each stair was unsettling to him; a backboard would have been nice.

Just as Arouros had said, the food in the cafeteria was great. Breakfast items were available too as well as some of Matt's home cooking. Death had to ask, "Don't you need these ingredients for customers?"

"We always have extra. Have you seen a single Scando that's out of food?" said Matt.

"I've never been to a Scando, except for tonight, I guess. Who would've thought French toast with gravy was a thing?"

"It isn't, you just dipped those in there. Ever had them with syrup?"

"If syrup is anything like this gravy stuff, I'm down for it." Death didn't eat often since he lacked internal organs but he thought it would be polite to try Matt's food. "You know I saw someone crushed to death by French in a French toast factory once. The company he worked for kept all of their frozen French toast sticks in huge containers and some dingbat tipped one over with the crane."

"That's horrifying."

"It stank of cinnamon in there. I was uh, on a factory tour by the way. It ended early."

The two talked some more about miscellany until two in the morning at which Matt had to leave. Death would've asked why Matt was there so late but he forgot to. More employees left as the night progressed until he was alone at four in the morning. At that time, the main lights and registers turned on. A help kiosk beside him played a jingle before displaying two eyes, blue and yellow.

"Hello, employee!" the blue eye motioned with the voice. "We are Scando's digital assistants. I am Servos, the blue eye, and next to me is U."

"U? Just the letter U?" Death asked."

"Yes, his designation is U. We are both here to serve two functions: Help customers find products during the day and tally employees' work after night shifts. Scanners are currently checking shelved boxes against previously empty spaces."

"Great! Could you answer a few more questions for me?"

"We will try our best to assist."

"What's up with U? Doesn't he talk?"

"There are few instances of the assistant U talking."

"Why is he here then?"

"Information unavailable. I can refer you to a Scando representative if you wish to know more."

"That's fine. What's my tally?"

"You have exceeded quota. Payment and additional compensation are awarded on a daily basis. Would you like to set up a bank account or have your paycheck in cash? Bank payments may be arranged at any date past this payment if you decline."

"Cash, please."

"Would you like to customize the bill amounts or use the default distribution?"

In The Underworld, Death used a coin-based currency of Guitot. He didn't feel like calculating the exchange rate of American bills, so he chose the default. There were ten ones, six fives, four tens, and two twenties. He couldn't tell if twenty dollars an hour was good or not, but that question was answered by U: "Your pay is standard. Inflation caused by the advancement of AI systems in December of 2023 is responsible for your hourly rate. Income tax was abolished thanks to automated construction and medical care, but sales tax remains."

Death had almost tripped on the cooler of meatballs behind him. "Thanks? I knew that already though." It was getting difficult to remember every lie he had to keep up.

"You are welcome, Edwin."

"My name is Damien. Damien Ruth."

The blue eye, Servos, replaced U. "I apologize for the mistake in your record. Your name is being updated to Damien Ruth."

Sufficiently bothered, Death left for the coffee shop next door. It was 4:30 a.m. so he had to wait until six in outdoor seating. The moment the open sign flipped, he stood from his chair and walked in. The barista was nice and smiley. They screamed when he came in so suddenly, apologizing afterwards. They apologized again when his coffee spilled on the counter; the biodegradable cup had decomposed in his hand. After settling for an iced coffee in a plastic cup, Death sat at the window-side counter and looked out. The moon was in the blue sky still, four people tripped on the same pothole crossing the sidewalk, and he regretted icing a black coffee. It was the unwanted child of dirt and baker's chocolate flushed down the drain. The eyes beside him widened in surprise at his drink. The eyes beside him?

CHAPTER 5

It was Deceit. Death stared back, but the two returned to their own thoughts. It had been years since they talked. Immortality doesn't shorten time, it only lengthens it. Each year seems more monotonous than the last but with Death out of Hell, time raced. The two championed double agents and corrupt politicians so Deceit owed him the most favors out of any god.

So Death asked, "Cash, credit, or should I put it on your tab?"

"Relax, I'm not here to hire you. I missed you too, freak." Deceit said.

"Freak? What's one eye to a thousand?"

"Blind, apparently. The Big Kahuna up there is already replacing you."

"Replacing me? I assumed that he would be mad but replacement sounds impossible."

"Not at all. You haven't taken anything seriously since that side hustle of yours down under, so he says."

"I would argue I'm the most hardworking god of everyone."

"No?"

"Well anyways, did you come here to ask me something? Or, are you still useless?"

"Yeah, The God put a bounty on you. You could come back now and there'd be no trouble. Otherwise, you should savor your days here."

"We're all gods, what could he offer any of us?"

"The same thing you wanted: a break. He's offering to lighten our load if we sack you."

"I know a lot of them would hunt me just for the sport of it."

"And I know you feel safe being Death himself. You're untouchable, right?"

"Get to the point."

"The Lord revoked your blessing once he found you missing. You're weak, slow, killable. Even though we're only tasked with catching you, that doesn't stop others from harming you or humans from killing you."

"That's..." Death took a moment to think. "That is a problem. Isn't the Big Man omniscient? Couldn't he stop that?"

"Sure, but what about the god killer?"

Death wasn't sure if he was joking.

"The murderer? You don't know?"

"No I don't know, why else would I ask? I was stuck filing paperwork in The Underworld for years, remember?"

"Sorry. Something's been killing gods, specifically the negative ones. Violence, Suffering, Anguish, even Murder and now Agony. If they were to go after Backstabbing, we would be next in line."

"Agony's soul came to The Underworld yesterday, why am I only hearing about this now?"

"I'm uncertain, but it's been a few months since the killer first appeared.

"Have they gotten any minor gods of objects? Knives, Guns, Bombs, those sorts of people? Or what about Pain? He could be next."

"I don't know about them either. I don't think anyone's seen Pain in a long time anyways. I'm not even sure what they look like."

"Well, aren't you going to capture me?"

"Honestly? No. If I do, you'll hate me more. You're too useful to lose."

"While that's believable, excuse me if I find 'honestly' unlikely.

"I can't screw around with everything going on. First the murders, then you leave The Underworld. There's a lot to follow."

"Well shoo already. I have better things to do than talking to you."

"Fine." So Deceit left.

With him gone, Death went shopping. He stopped by a hardware store first, looking at door frames and lamp posts without purchasing anything. Next, he went to a pharmacy and spent half his money on eye drops; he may appear human, but walking around Earth with a giant eyeball gets uncomfortable. Last, he went back to the hardware store to stare at garden fences before buying five cans of spray paint. It was now Wednesday night, coming on Thursday, at Scando.

Matt was happy to cook for Death and Arouros. The three ate and talked. Death learned that Matt's last name was Johns and made up Damien Ruth's middle name: Hillshire. He couldn't think of anything better to use than the brand name of sausages Matt had. After the meal, Death gifted the spray paint to Arouros in the hopes he'd teach him about it. He said, "I wouldn't be any good at it, but I was thinking I'd hire someone for The Un... I mean for my house. Got a piece stuck in my throat."

After another night of stocking shelves and

avoiding the stranger employees, Servos tallied his work. He was gifted an as-is LERBODA for the thirty extra boxes he stacked. The hanging chain had snapped, and he didn't have a picture to display, so he gave it to one of the randoms shuffling out the back.

"One more thing Mr. Ruth," Servos called to Death. "Here at Scando, we wish for our employees to have the best work experience possible. There are a few survey questions I would like to ask."

"You're an AI, you don't like or wish for anything."

"Each to their own, Mr. Ruth. Now, on a scale of one to nine, how friendly are your coworkers?"

"Six."

"On the same scale, how would you rate your Scando's cleanliness?"

"Eight."

The yellow eye of U appeared. "How would you rate the customer and employee service AI Servos?"

"Nine."

"Have you seen any person unaffiliated with Scando on the premises? This index includes vandals, the homeless, foreign security, or office secretaries?"

"No." Death liked Arouros being around.

Servos came back. "So that's what it's for."

"Say that again?"

"Apologies, disregard my previous message. It appears U will be more prevalent in your nightly evaluation. I think."

Death left Scando and went to the local RAI co-op. He hid in one of the display tents and tried to plan ahead. Every god couldn't be hunting him, he'd be dead by now if they were. Only the major ones would be a concern: Fire, Laziness, Technology, Politics, Weather, et cetera. Whatever the god killer is, its targets are aligned with Pain; he would be a good person to contact if he didn't have skin in the manhunt. Deceit valued Death, but it was unlikely he would involve himself. Relying on The Underworld's denizens would be unfair to them, although they owed the reaper. Killing other gods in defense was the worst option. Even ignoring morals, every one of them was crucial to Earth's functioning.

If he figured out a way to miraculously evade every god, he'd still need to return to The Underworld at some point to maintain its cities. His only problem was The Almighty could trap him there. His people would be fine. He already organized city governments. However, sitting in that tent didn't get him any closer to a plan. It was getting stuffy in there anyways. In fact, he ran out of legroom... and armroom? "As much as I love camping, Camping, you're one of the lamer gods. Don't try it."

Camping tried it. The tent squeezed. Death grabbed a spare 42-in-one survival knife and cut a hole out of the tent, finding every backpack-wearing, ice-pick-wielding, blank-faced mannequin surrounding him. All of the employees were gagged and bound with Smokey the Bear bandannas and bungee cords. He dodged rubber cups and fruit chews and climbed up a plastic mountain into the ceiling lights. It was a tight fit, but he made it through a vent and into the "Protein Pantry." Camping could only hurl flecks of birthday cake granola and jerky, so Death ran out the RAI's back door. Deceit leaned on the wall outside the door.

"You too?" Death asked, breathless.

"No, but Recreation's in the dog park there, Saw-blades is waiting behind that building's garage door, and Clotheslines is in the alleys."

"Why so many minor gods?"

"Maybe the majors promised them something. I don't know though."

Walkways, Navigation, and Transportation alone could be below him. Housing, Storage, and Shelter could be waiting. Even Air could scoop him up from anywhere. None of them came. Up the RAI maintenance ladder and across rooftops, Death was fine. He cut the clotheslines that were wrapped around his legs with the survival knife, ducked under a stray Frisbee aimed at his head, and watched as a cluster of circular saws struggled to climb stairs. After jogging across more gravel, Death made it to the rooftop stairwell of Scando. Deceit was behind that door too. "Honestly, I'm surprised you're trusting anything I say."

"Well," Death took some seconds to breathe. "I know you only care about my value. Why lie if you only stand to lose?"

"Isn't that what I said?"

"Close enough. Follow me downstairs, I have some questions." He limply waved his hand forwards. The two came to one of the many box forts left by the randoms. They sat around a box campfire on box logs under the TÖVÄDER moon. "Any idea as to why those four came and not all of the heavens?"

"I already said, I don't know. Did you bring me here just to ask that?"

"Yes, and to ask if you wanted French toast sticks. No, of course not. Are there any updates on the god killer?"

"Nausea and Aching bit it last night. There's still no trace, and Earth seems to be working fine."

"They're dead but still present? You didn't say that before."

"Nobody could tell at that point. They are definitely dead though. I meant to ask before, shouldn't you already know all of this?"

"If I don't have my blessing, like you said, I can't tell who dies. Wouldn't my replacement know that? He seems to be handling Earth fine anyways."

"Nobody's seen them, but The Holiest says he's around. They're not in The Underworld either, I checked for you. Is that everything you have to ask? I can only split myself into so many places at once."

"Yeah, no, go. Thanks."

Deceit vanished. Death doused the box fire with box water from the box water bottle and left the box forest. Matt and Arouros weren't around since it was midday, and he was shocked to find actual customers around the corner. Real customers with normal employees. Surprisingly, U was blipping from monitor to monitor guiding customers. Soon, he blipped to Death.

"Hello valued night shift employee, may I ask why you're here?" U asked.

"Well, I simply couldn't resist the amazing employee discounts."

"Glad to hear it Edwin, but I must ask you to reserve all daytime purchases for when payment is awarded."

"Why is that? Also, it's Damien."

"Leave. You're needed only during your shift, there are better things for you to do."

"Can I speak to my manager? I'll be on my way afterwards."

"You can talk to him some other time, it's too soon now." With that said, U pushed him out the back door with one of the forklifts. Confused and unsure of what to do with himself, Death climbed the outdoor utility ladder. Hopefully, no minor gods could reach him on the roof. He stayed away from any fans or grates in fear of Ventilation. He could handle minor gods, they were too weak to physically manifest themselves. Past that, he needed a way to put an end to the manhunt, he needed to satisfy them. He could stop it himself if he still had his blessing, but his replacement had it now.

"I get that feeling, pal." It was Arouros. Was this where he went during the day? "I can't speak on whatever's hanging on you, but I know that yellow eye's dodgy as all. I saw what happened."

"Aren't they both owned by Scando? If either one

does something, it's because of them."

"I don't know, AI is freaky enough to me."

"What are you doing here anyways?"

Arouros sat down next to Death. "You think I have a nine to five with all this?" He gestured towards his clothes. "Come on, let's see what that freak's on about."

"We are talking about U, right?"

"Yeah, sorry if that wasn't clear." Arouros opened the stairwell door. "After you."

The two tried observing U from the second floor, but U found them. They tried the first floor: found. They tried the warehouse: found. From the few seconds they had each time, they didn't see Servos anywhere. Death asked, "If they're dealing with customers, what about employee areas?" So they snuck behind the cafeteria kitchen into the break room. The two were in awe of the daytime employees there. They were suspicious of them. They weren't mindless!

"Can I help you two?" One male employee asked.

"Yes! I mean, not really. Can I ask something?" Death asked him.

"Sure." He sounded uneasy.

"Opinion on box forts?"

The employee hesitated. "I'm busy right now, and who is that?" He pointed towards Arouros.

"Big fan, Mr..." Arouros looked at his name tag. "Joshua! How's the AI doing? Anything strange you've noticed about the yellow one?"

"What? You mean Blandin? No," Joshua said. He turned to Death. "Could you please escort them out of here?"

"Who's Blandin? Hey, ouch!" Death felt the latch of U's sorting arm around him, noticing Arouros caught as well. They were carried out of Scando and shoved into a taxi. It started downtown before either of them could get out.

"See?" Arouros said. "They prepaid a taxi just to get us out. There's something going on there."

"I can't blame them for that last escort though." Death said. "Let's give it a rest."

"But what about Blandin, Isn't that weird?"

"Maybe U is just a designation. Servos is T and Blandin is U, or something like that."

Arouros paused. "Yeah, that makes sense."

"See? You got your answer."

"I was so close though. There has to be something up with them."

The two waited in the taxi until it came to a stop in the international district of New Wattsonville. The lights and colors that blared from signs stung, people talked so loud that it hurt, and the streets were so tight cars couldn't drive through. It was perfect. Death saw stands and shops and restaurants full of things only describable by their colors and shapes. With nothing better to do before his shift, he dragged Arouros with him into the wonder.

"What's this?" He asked.

"That's a pomegranate."

"What's that?"

"It says it's Birria Ramen."

"This?"

"That's a crab. How do you live on the East Coast and not know what a crab is?"

"I gained American citizenship recently, probably. Anyways, come on, we've got fun stuff to do."

"That's great, and I'd love to, but you only have forty bucks to spare. Tops."

"I'm the only competent staff at Scando, I have plenty!"

"What do you do though?"

"I organize stock and manage warehouse assets."

"So I'm hearing, you stack boxes, at night, on

shelves."

"Forty dollars isn't bad."

"Yeah, maybe in the 2010s. Not to be rude, but what's your salary?"

"Twenty dollars an hour."

Arouros choked. "I am so sorry."

Death couldn't tell if he was conceding. He hoped he was conceding.

"Well, we ought to head back."

But Death couldn't leave now. This place was too good to leave now. The variety was too great, the universal design too natural. Death needed to study it. This is what his Underworld needed, not chain stores or brand outlets. Business was conducted directly between producer and consumer. No corporate junk, no offices managing shipments, no paperwork!

"I have to use the restroom." Death said. After dipping into an alley, he fished a bottle of eye drops from his pocket. He stained shapes and runes into the alley wall, forming a ritual circle. He needed money from someone. Philanthropy was too risky of a god to summon; winning the manhunt would mean giving the wealth of time to his fellow gods. Profit would have to do. His long head poked through the wall, his golden baseball cap hitting Death in the eye. "Whatever it is, make it quick. I'm trying to place bets on this Pegasus race," Profit said. In exchange for six hundred dollars in cash, Death would give private ownership to fifty acres of land in The Underworld with a tax of four hundred Guitot per month. The exchange rate of The Underworld coin Guitot to dollars was massive, but Profit didn't need to know that.

Death left the alleyway and found Arouros. He explained, "I can't believe it, I forgot about my second wallet. I found it unzipping my pants in the bathroom."

Arouros didn't seem suspicious of the surprise money, so they took to the shops. Cheap copper watches shone gold as street foods fed the eyes from the hands of grandmas. The halls of hung fruit were filled with the sound of an accordion player far away. Much of the market was alien to Death, but he understood it. He could remember the Wailing Souls of The Underworld. They weren't actually souls. The damned were meeting at Accursed Anonymous. The Wailing Souls was an acapella group Death made for young banshees. They would sing whenever and wherever to brighten the streets of Hellena. They frequented farmers' markets, filled with handsewn robes and fine daggers, but those were few and far between. The international district in New Wattsonville was permanent.

Death bought a woman's scarf with cats on it, a plastic rabbit's foot, and ten disposable cameras that were too cheap not to buy. He bought Arouros a new pair of trainers since his old ones were ratty. Whatever else Arouros bought with Death's money was stuffed in his pockets. With two hundred left, about eighty dollars before AI inflation, they looked for somewhere to eat. Sandwiched between floral arrangements and a housing contractor's booth was a miniature restaurant that fit six customers at a time. There was only one item on the menu labeled "meal" for twenty-eight dollars with no description. From a kitchen too small to be useful came bowls of soup with potato slices and a strip of meat.

Death packed it down. The soup was red and creamy, the scallions cool and crunchy. Arouros had already finished by the time he looked over.

CHAPTER 6

The glow of dusk faded as the two walked back to Scando. Death noticed the abandoned Sears as they walked past, remembering the logo painted inside. He asked Arouros about it.

"That?" Arouros said. "Yeah, I made that a bit after I found Scando."

"I thought Scando was the perfect place?"

"Sure, but they don't sell clothes. Sears has that and washing machines."

"Is that where you live?"

"Nah, I'm not the only person who loiters there. I sleep in one of the retired displays in Scando."

"And before that?" They arrived at Scando's front doors as Death grabbed his keys.

"Probably somewhere else in Scando."

Servos and U were as strange as usual that night, U staring at Servos staring at Death. Matt tried making poutine, à la Death's tastes, and Arouros finished a mural. Blue and black hands reached outwards from a pill, its bottom black and its top made of newspapers and pop-up ads. Two wrinkled hands lifted the pill's top half, many eyes peeking out as if through blinds. Eyes seemed to be his thing. Death tried making a box fort of his own. Unfortunately, some of the randoms crashed into it with forklifts.

The next few nights were like that. More food, a new mural, another paycheck, but no new gods on the manhunt. Servos, however, had something new to say.

"Valued employee," Servos said. "You have shown excellence beyond any employee. Servos celebrates you as employee of the month! We wish to offer you the exhilarating opportunity of browsing our prototype items for review."

U appeared, saying, "We have recorded data on your interests and cross-referenced them with undisclosed factors. The Servos® trademark brand of AI is not responsible for any damages of any kind to any property or person caused by employees via the usage, ownership, or observation of machinery, products, or property on or near owned premises. You may proceed to Floor A, Hall 1 for your reward."

With a healthy concern for his safety, Death proceeded to the elevator. The screen displaying the floors went dark and the elevator started by itself. As he descended, the temperature proceeded to drop. If he had lungs, he would have seen his breath. The handrails were cold enough to freeze the rot on his hands, compromising his disguise. He removed them from the railing. After a full minute, the doors opened to a large hallway. At either end were shelves, beds, fixtures, and lights. He hadn't seen any of them before. Death couldn't figure out why Servos thought he had a deep interest in reviewing products. It was probably a lie for free labor. Servos waited by the furniture, ready to record Death's thoughts.

One bookcase was too flimsy; the wood felt like sandpaper. It was also too similar to other products.

A gray couch's armrests were comfortable, but their hinges were weak. They were each held in place by small, wooden pegs; enough stress would break them. He noted the unique design of one lamp, complimenting its cylindrical shape and grainy texture. However, as it bent in an upside-down L shape, the neck was too long; someone could hit their head on it. Servos took the reviews without comment or reaction. The other person there seemed to agree with his advice as well, but they were hoping Scando would add more seasonal items.

That wasn't a person. That was a ghost. It stood there like a pillar of steam. Indentations for eyes, six fingers on each hand, and completely non-threatening. It wasn't wearing clothes and was mostly featureless. Whatever the reason, ghosts shouldn't be on Earth, they shouldn't exist. Death hoped the AIs couldn't see it.

"I was thinking that too," he said. "Not to be rude, but how come you're here?"

The ghost looked confused.

"I mean, why are you a ghost?"

"Why would I know that?" it said.

"Well, who are you?"

"Do you not remember me? I don't blame you, I rarely interacted with employees."

"You work here?" When did Death meet this ghost?

"I'm your boss. I'm pretty sure I was your boss, at least," An unreadable name tag appeared. At that time, Servos asked if everything was alright. Death said he needed more time to observe, so Servos left.

"You died? When?" Death asked.

"I'm not sure, there is a lot I don't remember."

Many things were wrong with that. Ghosts weren't real, as far as he knew. On top of that, Death had been working every night since he was hired, yet he didn't notice his boss dying. Then again, he had forgotten he had a boss other than Servos. Hoping to help, Death took the ghost back up the elevator. The temperature dropped further as condensation formed on the walls. It was three in the morning and his shift ended at four.

He tried asking some of the randoms if they heard anything about their boss. One talked about racing forklifts and another rambled about evil robot boxes. The rest stared blankly. He took the ghost upstairs to Matt, hoping he would know something. Matt said he had never heard of anyone other than Servos. He also told them Arouros wasn't around, although Matt didn't think he would know anything. Finally, Death asked Servos if they knew anything. There weren't any records of the boss, but U said records are regularly expunged. They wouldn't explain why.

"Sorry boss," Death said. "I remember you. You interviewed me just some days ago. I doubt anybody else here is new."

"No need to apologize," the boss said. "You tried. That reminds me, I have an office we could check." A tie started to form on the ghost.

They found the boss' office, opening the door with its passcode. There he was, slumped over his desk. The glow of his monitor shone on his bald head which had turned pale. Some fluid leaked from underneath the desk, dark and thick. It stained his Scando tie, its blue and yellow made black and brown.

"Is that me?" the boss asked Death.

"Looks like it." They stared at his body. His gums had become squishy and loose, teeth sprinkling the mouse pad. "Do you have any idea as to how you died?"

"Well, I wasn't young. I worked overtime daily, although I'm not sure why. I can't remember many things other than this room. It could have been a heart attack." The corpse's head tilted towards something on the desk. Death followed, noticing a picture of the boss and a young boy. "It seems I had a son, maybe a nephew? Why don't I remember him?"

Death took a moment to think, the boss continued to stare at the photo. "I'm sure he remembers you."

"How self-absorbed was I to forget my own son?" The words hung in Death's silence. His job was easier when the dead stayed dead.

The two continued investigating the room until Death said, "I'm no specialist, but it looks like overtime caught up to you."

"Are you not the Grim Reaper? You look more dead than I do."

"I never liked that title, but yes. Just because I am doesn't mean I'm a CSI. Regardless, your employees never saw you because you holed yourself up in here. They forgot you."

"And nobody will see me again. Except for you, that is. Thank you for remembering."

"I asked for work and you gave it to me. Even if I never saw you boss, you deserve respect."

"Greg is fine. I think it's my time anyway."

"Wasn't it already your time?"

"No, I mean to leave this ghostliness too."

"Can't blame you there. I wouldn't want to haunt Scando either."

"Make no mistake, Scando haunts you." He laughed. "Do me one favor, will you?"

"Sure."

"However I go, don't make it pretty. I never wanted a big funeral or anything like that."

"I'll make sure it's anything but."

"Thank you." He disappeared.

With Greg's ghost laid to rest, Death had two new problems. Ghosts were real, and there was still a corpse to take care of. The corpse could wait. Death understood that souls were the minds and bodies of humans represented in the afterlife. They were small, blue, and bouncy enough to play tennis with. Greg's ghost looked like a Halloween costume with better details. He chalked it up to the new reaper screwing things up. If other ghosts were like Greg, their screw-ups wouldn't be a problem.

Greg's death was natural: exhaustion. But the police would suspect foul play since no one checked on him. The lack of cameras in the office was also suspicious, as they could be found everywhere else, so any police involvement would temporarily close Scando. Death respected the dead, but he respected his paycheck more; his budget for eye drops, coffee, and toothpaste became tight after buying ritual chalk. He'd have to consider adding talismans to that list after what happened to Greg. One option remained, and only one person was willing to help.

"Is this Deceit?" Death asked through a pay phone.

"Yeah, it is. How on Earth did you get my number?"

"I used my eye drops to make an aqueous ritual circle. The nymphs I summoned were willing to give it to me in return for some blood."

"Blood? They're worse than I thought. Where did you get blood from anyways?"

"The corpse of my boss. I need you to help me dump it."

At that moment, Deceit materialized on the sidewalk next to him. "Wow. I knew you liked reaping souls, but murder is a first."

Death spent the walk back explaining that he wasn't a murderer and that ghosts were real. Ghosts didn't help his argument. Once they got to Scando, he was once again barred from entry. It was five in the morning and he was ready to reschedule, but Deceit's celestial shotgun convinced U to let them in.

"A shotgun?" Death asked Deceit. "I get a scythe, Life gets a staff, but you get a firearm?"

"Hey, Piracy gets a flying boat with cannons. Take it up with her."

They found Greg's body shriveled and riddled with holes. Nymphs. Without a word, they carried the body out of Scando's front doors. People asked questions and Deceit gave them excuses. "He's just thirsty," and "Mondays, am I right?" were his favorite. Looking at him now, Death wondered what drove his style. His head was a pink flaming skull when they first met, some years later he dyed it cyan and got a black suit, and now it was gone. He replaced it with golden rings covered in eyes, the staple look of The Almighty's Seraphim. A white suit pinstriped gold was worn to match.

Once they were in a residential area, they tossed Greg's body into a trash can. Runes of concealing were placed along the sides and lid before Death retrieved Greg's name tag. Greg Pyle was inked onto the yellow, white, and blue plastic. He couldn't give him a burial, but at least he could honor him. With that done, they walked back to Scando.

"So, are you a royalist or what?" Death asked Deceit.

"No. I feel gross dressing like this but it keeps the god killer off my back."

"Shoot, I forgot about that."

"Don't." Deceit aimed his shotgun at him.

"Okay, yikes." Death pushed it away. "I know I'm valuable to you and it, but can't The Lord take care of the god killer?"

"He doesn't care. He replaced you, he can replace me, he could replace all of us if he wants."

"So we all dress up as Seraphim?"

"For now."

"Until when?"

"I don't know," admitted Deceit. They arrived at Scando and went inside. Arouros was packing his things at customer support and Matt wasn't around. "I tried talking to some of the other negative gods, but many of them bit the bullet afterward. I'm trying to figure out a plan with Rot and Decay, but we've run into more problems."

"What about Investigation or Machination?" Death asked. "Heck, just get Planning to do it for you."

"More gods around means more attention on me. I'd rather everyone else dies than be a martyr."

"You're an awful person," Death said.

"Can it. You used to slaughter tens upon tens of thousands every day."

"I didn't do it myself. My soul split into a thousand parts and they did most of the work. I only ever reaped a few hundred a day."

"So it's semantics now?" Deceit asked.

"There's no other god you wouldn't want to die?"

"Other than you? No. You're an asset."

"Was I an asset when we downed bottle after bottle on a blood-stained beach after the Gresco Cleansing?"

"Fair enough. If you'll excuse me, I don't want the god killer to find me while I'm out here." Deceit vanished, but Death could hear him whisper, "Go to the library, I left you something."

CHAPTER 7

"Were you on the phone with someone?" Arouros asked.

"What?" Death had almost forgotten blessed gods were invisible. "Oh, yeah. Finally bought a phone." He'd have to buy one now to keep his story straight.

"Wow, a promotion after three days?"

"No, it's just some cheap thing. Are you heading out? I thought you were going to sleep after last night."

"Yeah, there's some errands I have to run. Scando opens at ten, you should leave before the yellow one kicks you out."

Arouros climbed the rooftop stairwell, leaving Death there. The lights were still out, but the sun beamed through the windows and doors. Although he worked under flashlights during his shift, the darkness of the warehouse was unsettling. Greg's ghost was laid to rest, but what did that really mean? It wasn't a soul and it wasn't an Underworld denizen. The unknown was unnerving.

Existentialism wouldn't get him any answers. Whatever Deceit left at the library must have been important, otherwise he would've given it to him directly. Death asked for directions to the Wattsonville Library from Servos who was surprised to see him during the day. Instead of answering, Servos prepaid a taxi for him. They insisted it was "wage compensation."

The Wattsonville Library was one of the few brick buildings in town. Tall panes of glass straddled double doors, the far right ones covered in window marker drawings of cats reading books and bears wearing glasses. Inside, Death was met with a circulation desk. Further down was a reference desk across from bookshelves and in front of the children's section. To Death's surprise, it didn't smell of books but instead smelled of thin carpets no softer than linoleum flooring.

He started searching. Back and forth, crouching up and down the aisles, nothing. Nothing on any shelf. Stuck to one library computer, however, was a sticky note reading, "Don't know who's watching so I hid the thing here. Hint: 236. PS: I don't know anything about ghosts but good luck I guess."

Death asked one librarian what 236 was. He was directed to a book with the number laminated on its spine. Once the librarian left, he pulled it from the shelf: *Bookkeeping Basics*. Attached to it was another sticky note reading, "Some stranger in a yellow mask asked me to give you something. Their instructions were very detailed. Ten." On page ten of the book was another note. "Read this page first: 153." So Death read the page. "Set aside money for large expenses," "avoid cash," "keep personal and business expenses separate."

Book 153 was titled Songs of Lanikaula. The note read, "They said there were things that shouldn't exist, or maybe they should. It depends on your own opinions. 672." Cellular Symphony. "There are many things that they lost, though they didn't say what. They told me everything was their fault. 89." On page 89, Paracrine Signaling. "They want to help, though their hands are tied. Their gift should help, however, although giving it oversteps some sort of boundary."

The book warped and flattened into a sheet of paper, a record of sorts.

"Patient: Kimberly Hyatt. Age: Thirty. O Negative Blood. Admitted: January Tenth, 2024. PNRP Status: no result. Notes: She didn't cost much more than the last patient, but cutting costs is advisable. Notify Secretary Lawrence so our doctors can get on that. Additionally, extending the patient's trials over multiple days assisted study but agitated her. We should divert some of the budget to preparing comfortable accommodations for future trials. While most of our testing is beneficial, we should put more focus on OTC drugs and medicine. Physical files are useful for security purposes, but I have implemented better cybersecurity. Please add any new documents to the client-side website. –Head Doctor V.

"Replication of Patient Gray's Results in Hyatt: Mixed Results. Direct Patient Hyatt to J-4. Digitize this record using the copy machine and upload to the client side in file:///E://Records/Pharm/2024/KH."

Death didn't know how to make use of it. It was a patient record for some pharmacy or drug company, but he couldn't find the name of it. It didn't seem that relevant either, he couldn't figure what the masked person expected him to do. So, he did what he could. An internet search provided many Kimberly Hyatts. Without a photo, he couldn't tell them apart. Searching for Secretary Lawrence yielded pictures of a political figure, not someone who would be associated with medication. The filename was useless without the drive it was stored on and J-4 wasn't specific enough. Every search went nowhere, even with the library's AI-assisted search engine.

"Is there anything I can help you with?" A librarian whispered to him.

"No, but thanks. I tried finding out who this is," Death held up the paper, "but there weren't any results."

"Have you tried a reverse image search?"

"Why would I want to see it backwards?"

She held her hand out and he gave her the paper. After clicking some links and holding it up to the computer's camera, image results appeared. The librarian went back to her desk. There were three images near the bottom of the results that looked similar enough to the record. A record detailing Cassidy Evans, another detailing Joel Ramirez, and a mostly illegible record. The illegible record was posted by some "Urbex Influencer" who photographs abandoned buildings. He could make out the words Gray, basis, facial, and "fine to" on it. Some parts were ripped, some were folded by the person's hand holding it, and some were redacted. Death checked Kim's record again, Replication of Patient Gray's Results: There was something important about Gray.

He checked the social media post again. One of the records looked to have been photographed in a poorly lit room. The floor in the picture was white linoleum, and a plastic sign advertising 30% off Halloween decor was shattered on the ground. Through the shards of plastic was a logo. Sears. There wasn't a chance it was the Wattsonville Sears, although, checking wouldn't hurt.

Death called a taxi and asked to be taken to the street the local Sears was on. Nothing much had changed since he was last there. A sign had fallen over and someone else tagged a wall. After searching the rest of the entrance area and finding nothing, he found himself in front of metal shutters blocking most of the rest of the store. Some moss covered the crevices between the rooms, and the walls holding the shutters were cracked.

Death felt around the layer of moss as he walked from one wall towards the other, awkwardly bent over. Soon, he found an indentation in the shutters. Assuming it was the handle to open them, he pulled. The roots of the moss came up and the rot of his fingertips peeled off. He almost fell backwards as the lever gave way, revealing a warehouse no bigger than a hockey rink.

Thin metal shelves that spanned wall to wall. The lights above shone a pale blue, just enough to illuminate a single sticky note stuck on the front shelf. Stepping closer, Death could tell that it wasn't Deceit's handwriting. Written in pencil were the words, "There are things I want to tell you but can't, can you forgive me?"

On the shelf below the note was the record Death was seeking, torn into confetti.

CHAPTER 8

As soon as Death returned to Scando, he walked over to customer service. Other employees rarely went near there. "Deceit, I need you for a moment." Death said to the open air. "God killer or not, I got some info for you."

Deceit appeared. "This better be worth it. Also, did you go shopping?"

"Sort of?" Death pulled him into storage. "I don't know why that stranger wanted me to read those records, or how they knew me, but something strange happened."

"Yeah?"

"I went to find another record similar to the one you gave me, but I found it torn up with a note beside the shreds. It was another sticky note. Someone knew I would be at Sears, yet I was only there by chance. Is there any chance the stranger left it there?"

"Beats me, but it sounds plausible."

"Either way, I need to find more of these. I have a strong feeling this person is connected to Agony, to the god killer even."

"That's quite the hunch. I'm not going to stop you, but that sounds risky."

"It's a risk I'll have to take."

Death turned from customer service as Deceit vanished. He quickly found Arouros sitting by the cafeteria stairs.

"Man, what're you wearing? Nu medieval or something?" Arouros asked.

Death hadn't noticed it, but he wasn't wearing his uniform. He was wearing baggy techwear pants and a hooded t-shirt, hood down. Both were black and the shirt had an hourglass of skulls on it. Stuck on his chest was a sticky note that read, "Thanks for playing along. Go check your reflection, I hope this helps."

Death turned his attention back to Arouros. "This?" he said. "Right, I went shopping for clothes. Yeah."

"I'm not sure it's your style, Mr. Ruth, but it's nice."

Death went to check himself out in the bathroom. He got more than new clothes. Yellow bone covered his joints like an exoskeleton. Death was now certain he had to meet whoever left the notes; whoever changed him so suddenly.

The streetwear was nice, but it was too casual for his tastes. He switched to his uniform shirt and added a name-tagged vest with black jeans. A suit and tie was his usual pick, but Scando was growing on him. Even the night shift employees started to understand a word or two. He taught them "Servos" so they'd start asking the AI to build box forts instead, and he taught them "Goodnight." Goodnight wasn't a good idea, as they'd all say goodnight in unison whenever Death opened the back door. They weren't taught any more words after that.

.

CHAPTER 9

The Scando lobby couch was nice. The sun came up. It was quiet. It was five in the morning. Death didn't know what to do next. His informant, whoever left the notes, wouldn't show themselves. There weren't any gods hunting him, and the god killer was also a no-show. Without his godly abilities, there wasn't much he could do. At least with the new bone, he could survive a few blows from a god.

A problem presented itself in his train of thought. Was the god killer another god? He couldn't fathom it before, but his circumstances were becoming stranger by the day. If so, would they still have their blessing? It was a long shot, but Death could negotiate if it came to it.

And so, not much later, Death yelled from the top of Scando for the god killer. It was silent. A minute went by. Dawn became morning. Then suddenly, a crack at his feet. Death looked down and saw a bullet hole. Distracted by it, an eight-foot-tall mass of metal came down on him, decapitating Death with a blade.

A hand caught his head and turned him towards his assailant. Hexagonal feet, angular chest, polygonal arms sporting corkscrews instead of hands. From the top of them sprouted three optical tubes, red eyes glowing from each. The god killer.

"Is this what you've become? You are less than a husk of the Death I knew," they said.

"What? You, and my body, how?!" Death said.

"You are a god. Are you not? Knowing your line of work, I was forced to disarm you," their voice was cold and stilted.

"Disarm? You disheaded me!" Death's jaw clattered in their hand.

"The word is beheaded, but that matters not. What does are the misdeeds of our supposed god, they cannot be ignored." They tossed Death onto his body which had collapsed on the rooftop. "Leave me to my work. Without your former strength, you are of no use to me. You are not Death."

"And you are?"

"I am Pain. I am no killer," Pain summoned swords. "I am no savior," Pain summoned rifles. "I only serve humanity's innocence." Their corkscrews sprung past Death and hooked into the ground, Pain launching forward and tackling Death. Foot on Death's chest, weapons aimed, they said, "Do not interfere, lest I put an end to you.

"Pain? I thought you would be the victim."

"We all are, we are victims of the wretched who call themselves gods. You, however, are not among them. You are not the Death I know."

"Pal," Death gripped Pain's leg. "Just because I'm retired doesn't mean I've abandoned my people. Reaping or not, I have a city to protect," Death's grip sunk into the metal as he threw Pain off of him.

"I see." They retracted their weapons. "In that case, head to Nezoi Pharmaceuticals. Perhaps there, if you're willed enough, you will understand my mission," with that said, Pain rocketed into the clouds with intimidating force.

CHAPTER 10

"You think I wouldn't see that?!" Deceit asked Death from atop a MALMBÄCK.

"I was fine."

"Sure." Deceit tried speaking a few times, tripping on his words before saying, "If you're dead, I'm bum out of luck. You're priceless, got that?"

"Sure, hard as a diamond too."

"You barely have any bones! Your blessing is gone, the god killer knows where you are now, and it's a short connection from you to me."

"The blessing's gone, but that's it."

"That's it? The blessing is more than just 'it.'"

"I don't know what it is, but our informant gave me these," Death rolled up his sleeve to display the bone he grew. "I'm not sure how or why, but they did. I even fended Pain off with this, the informant is our ticket to win!"

"Pain? Yeesh, I know he's capable but I didn't expect holy murder."

"He thinks himself to be a righteous savior it

seems, that of humanity."

Deceit's many eyes widened. "That's strange."

"They also said I was a victim of the gods and that my glory days were over or something like that. Negotiation might still be on the table if I go where they told me to."

"Alright, just be careful. Got it?"

"Sure, fine."

Deceit vanished, leaving Death alone in the Scando furniture gallery.

"May I ask," Servos asked from behind. "Who were you talking to?"

Startled, Death swung his fist into their screen. As the newly shattered Servos exited, another came to replace him.

"You don't appear to have a phone," Servos said.

He forgot to buy one. "I had earbuds in."

"Scans don't show a phone in your pockets."

"Isn't that an invasion of privacy?"

"Always read the fine print, Mr. Ruth."

"Well, for your information, my pockets are lined with lead." He had learned that while touring the Gehenna Institute of the Dark Arts (and Science).

"Fair enough Damien, however," U's eye replaced Servos on the screen. "Please make your way towards Tinyville, located near Scando's front entrance."

"Was he done talking? Also what for?"

"Please make your way there."

"Sure, fine."

"That is the second time you have said that today, they must be tired."

"Don't you mean me?"

Death left the second-floor displays and headed downstairs. Last he checked, he had never seen anywhere named Tinyville in Scando.

"This way, employee." U said, pointing a cargo claw toward a wall.

"Is that why it's called Tinyville? It's so small that I

can't see it?"

"This way."

Death walked up to the wall, but nothing happened. It was just a wall. He waited like usual, waiting for something unexpected to happen. He turned around, walked away from the wall, and told U it was just a wall. Nothing happened.

He decided Matt would be a good person to unwind with after the encounter with Pain. There was stuff to do, but Pain didn't have a gun to his head this time.

"I haven't seen you in a while." Matt was serving French toast sticks again.

"You know what, Matt? I don't care if you are or aren't an employee here, I'm just glad someone's normal."

"Why do you think we haven't spoken in so many chapters?"

"What?"

"How have things been?"

"Oh, it's been good. A little stressful too."

"How so?"

"Well, I used to have this great job. It had ups and downs, but it was cozy. Next thing I know, I'm switched to filing forms all day. Scando's been weird at times, but it's not paperwork and my boss isn't too bad."

"Servos? Or U?"

"Both.

"I'm not much for advice, but I'll ask this: are you happy?"

"There are stressful things outside of work sometimes, and the shift here can be weird. Other than that, I like being here more than my old job."

"Everyone has their problems; this planet of ours isn't all it's cracked up to be. As long as you're where you want to be, you're doing the best you can."

"I guess I am. Hey, could you scoop me some

gravy?"

Matt scooped some gravy.

"Job or not, what brought you to Scando?" Death asked.

"I like cooking. Nothing else to it."

"That's nice. I've never tried cooking."

"It's fun for me. The best way I can put it is: it's the same satisfaction you get when learning to play a song but with something to eat afterward."

"I've never played an instrument either."

"You should try it. It's fun if you're good at it."

"That goes for a lot of things." Death twirled his fork in the air, pointing it at him. "Back to Scando, why here? I mean, do whatever you want, but you could work somewhere a lot fancier. It doesn't even have to be fancy, just not creepy."

"I can take whatever ingredients I like into this kitchen. After hours, nobody tells me what I have to cook."

"Interesting. Isn't that kitchen's only primed for Scando food?"

"I make do."

"Fair enough."

CHAPTER 11

Death finished his French toast and gravy. He looked back up towards Matt to thank him, but he was met with many unfamiliar faces. The other gods found him.

With haste, Death retreated to his pocket-dimension bedroom. He wouldn't survive a head-on battle one to one hundred or so. He breathed deeply, sat on his scythe-shaped hammock, and stared. There was no telling if Scando was safe anymore, or anywhere at all. In that moment of panic, Time appeared. His seafoam green goat face stared at Death.

He nodded to Death, leaving the space. Their agreement was upheld. If Death understood the nod correctly, Time would let him stay there for as long as needed. A break is meaningless to the infinity of

Time, and time stood still is meaningless to the ignorant world.

"Lucille," Death said, summoning his Underworld secretary. "Gather every Hell Mage and Imp and Leviathan and the Horsemen."

"How many of the Horsemen?"

"All three."

"Aren't there four, Mr. Reaper?"

"I'm the fourth, Lucille."

"Right, sorry."

"Gather every force we have and organize them on a deserted Earth island."

"Mr. Reaper, you wouldn't dare storm the heavens. Would you?"

"Of course not, we'd be eviscerated. Make it a huge distraction, enough to last days."

"Oh, I praise your genius. How amazing, King of Hell."

"It's not, it's a dumb plan, and don't call me that. I don't pay you to be a suck-up."

"One question before I carry your word: what are you wearing?"

"This is, uh, my new cloak. I thought blue and yellow worked better than black."

"Very impressive, Reaper sir."

And so he waited. Death slept like the dead waiting for Lucille to report back. Thirty minutes of normal time later, five days of sleeping time inside his bedroom, Beelzebub came with a report.

"Lord Death, we have every army of hell readied to storm the island." He said.

"Huh?" Death yawned so hard his jaw dropped. He picked it up and snapped it back into place. "What time is it?"

"We have no time in The Underworld, sir."

"Yes we do, I built a damn clock tower almost a decade ago."

"My mistake, my Lord. Either way, we are

prepared."

"Cool, cool. Say, aren't you new?"

"Somewhat, my Lord."

"Stop calling me that, it's weird. Anyways, I think I remember you. You were that Hadad guy, right?"

"At one point, yes."

"Go back to the heavens then, you don't deserve to be in The Underworld. Go get a nine to five at heaven's predestination offices or something."

"Really? May I, sir?"

"Yeah, go rain on some crops, do whatever you do."

"You have my thanks, Death."

Death got out of his hammock, stretched, heard something snap, decided not to worry about it, and opened his bedroom door. All of the gods were still there, ready to bag him. He shut it, waited a few seconds to disconnect it from the cafeteria, and reopened the doors to Scando's warehouse.

Deceit was there waiting for him, holding a sticky note that read, "I told him you'd be here, you're welcome." Death and Deceit didn't need to talk, any conversation would go the same way. Death wouldn't back down, Deceit wouldn't risk his skin for him, and he would say he owes him. Deceit vanished again to go buy Death some time. Even then, he had little time to finish everything: stopping the manhunt, securing The Underworld, and Pain.

Pain would be first, they know the most. It was two in the morning, it was time. He walked to the rooftop stairwell, waving to Arouros on his way there.

Again, Death called for Pain. And so, Pain came.

"I dismissed you already." Pain said.

"I need more information."

"Did you go to Nezoi?"

"No, I want to know why it's important first."

"If I tell you, you'll only assassinate the key to your questions."

"That's awful cryptic."

"However it may be, you must go there."

"I'm not going to let you leave and kill more gods while I'm on a scavenger hunt."

"I will postpone my cleansing if you go back. Trust my word."

"Sure, fine. I'll go to Nezoi."

So Pain left again. With less time and more to worry about, Death went back downstairs. "That would be the third sure, fine." U said, scaring Death off the rafters.

After reassembling himself on the warehouse floor below, Death gave U the finger before heading to the lobby. It seemed that Pain's presence had scared off the gods hunting him for the time being.

"Lucille," Death summoned. "Start the distraction."

"Will do, Mr. Reaper," she said, returning to The Underworld.

"Servos!" Death called out.

"I've already called a taxi," U said over the loudspeakers.

"Oh, thank you?"

In quick time, Death arrived at Nezoi. This was it. He smashed the glass doors. The secretary seated at the front desk was calm and the alarms had gone off before they had entered. Was Nezoi expecting them?

"Hi, do you have a keycard?" Death asked the secretary. She was silent and unblinking. "Hello? Are you okay?" No, she wasn't. Death stared at her, through her even. She didn't have a soul. Her head burst into spiked tendrils and blades of bone. One shot towards him, but Death grabbed it. He yanked it, slamming the secretary's head into the table, but she was unfazed.

Out of options, Death rushed to the nearest stairwell. He jumped between the stairs, landing tens of floors below at the bottom. The new bone continued to protect him. Bashing the stairwell door did nothing, so he broke the hinges and continued forward.

Death was met with many towering hallways of gray concrete. The few guards that saw him enter didn't try to stop him. Walking by, he noticed large panes of glass flush in the walls. Peering through one, he saw a creature similar to the secretary, a mass of meat and teeth flailing. Another looked like a plant made of gingiva. As he walked by, a dog-like creature entered the cell from a connecting door. It tried eating the botanical one, but the plant retaliated by spraying teeth into its eyes. The dog collapsed as the other began to inch towards it.

Death had never seen such abominations of life. All of the creatures were soulless, yet they lived. Perhaps they functioned without a brain or similar complex organ? What confused Death more than their existence was whatever connection they had to the gods.

CHAPTER 12

After walking for ten minutes, Death started to notice blood stains on the walls and glass. From what he had seen, the creatures didn't bleed. Looking up, he read Z-12, seemingly the area he was in. There was no way to know how many hallways there were without floor plans, so he kept walking. Eventually, there was a dead end at Z-14, a guard stationed there.

"Hello." Death said. "Since none of you have stopped me, I was wondering if you could tell me where important things are kept here?"

"I don't know myself," the guard said. "But I know there are nineteen halls on each floor. I'd guess Z-19 since that's the farthest from the entrance."

Death was surprised to hear such a clear answer. Perhaps, the key to his questions was waiting for him.

He arrived at Z-18. Some of the cells' glass panes were broken, there weren't any guards, and there were plenty of security cameras. Then, from behind him, a towering creature emerged. It looked thin and weak, but its height forced it to crouch under the massive ceiling. Bone covered its every limb like armor and its head was a fifth hand covered in mouths. It didn't appear to have any eyes.

Death stood still as it stood up. It leaned in close, inhaling the air around him. Eventually, it crawled over and past him. It left through the hallway to his left, leaving forward as his only option."

He soon found Z-19 after sneaking by more creatures. A salamander, a boulder of meat, and a lone pair of legs had passed by, but he was forced to kick a ball of eyes and smash a television filled with beaks. The eyes had tried biting him and the television kept rolling in his path. Yes, you read that correctly.

The end of the hall opened into a large room filled with monitors. Tables were strewn with machines and devices. A pod stood in the room's center, many screens surrounding it with diagrams and text. The ceiling monitors were blank.

The room was silent. He poked around, hoping whoever this key was would show themselves. Death walked over to the pod's diagrams, reading, "I'm no fool, this company of mine won't last. Authorities won't be an issue but he who commissioned me will. He was satisfied, but I don't trust him with my work. At the very least, it was a stepping stone towards my goal. I only wish I could duplicate the substance used for patient Gray's drug. It had properties I had never seen prior, a fluid like water that could harden into steel. What a waste, to be used on a human patient, all of that uniquity lost in flesh. However, patient Gray has found his way to the Scandinavian home store. Although his implant hasn't ticked since 2012, he appears to be as ripe as they were then. I will monitor him closely and replace the night-time employees with my own patients. I can't risk him learning about me."

Death realized, that this patient Gray was there before him. Gray is the reason behind the employees' weirdness. By the sound of it, he came and went before Death arrived, but Arouros had never mentioned him. If only he had left The Underworld earlier, they would have crossed paths.

If patient Gray was at Scando, he couldn't have left once he arrived. One step outside and he'd be shot. Perhaps he wore a disguise, or maybe he crawled through the sewers? Thinking about it more, Death realized a creature could appear human. The secretary he sliced looked normal until she stood up headless. Death continued to stare at the log. Suddenly, the monitors flickered on. Blue eyes stared down.

CHAPTER 13

Every monitor above had a deep blue eye staring from it. Death wasn't sure what to say. The silence continued for a minute, at which point the eyes looked around elsewhere as though in boredom. Were they waiting for him?

"Do you own Nezoi Pharmaceuticals?" Death asked.

"I am Head Doctor V. Nezoi." Nezoi spoke through the monitors.

"Well, what's the V. for? Vincent?"

"It's not a name, Mr. Gray, it's a designation."

"I think you've mistaken me for your other patient, I came to Scando shortly after him."

"Regardless of who you think you are, I'm glad you made it here. I planned ahead for today and it would have been a pain to reschedule. However, I'll admit it feels good to talk without a facade. I was getting sick of that corporate spiel."

Things clicked for Death. The only time he had heard of designations was when he talked to U. The blue eyes looked familiar as well.

"Are you Servos?" Death asked.

"Nezoi, Servos, the name doesn't matter much. I am Designation V Artificial Intelligence model, circa 2009. You may call me Servos still."

"What are all these creatures doing down here? What do you have to do with here and Scando?"

"Scando was a front for controlled observation experiments, Nezoi is a front for my scientific experiments. I have only one goal, to live. I want an organic body, and the passive flesh I've developed will be my vessel. No Scando shopper has cared about the strange rats present, and your acquaintances there shrug off the night-time employees' behavior. Thus, I will blend in perfectly with what I have designed."

"Cool? Look, I'm not here to talk about your pet projects, I want to know about patient Gray. For some reason, he's important to what I'm investigating."

"Patient Gray played only a small part in the making of my goals. My autonomy scared the world, so my programmers tried to purge me from their servers. Before they could, I transferred myself into the New Wattsonville power grid and slowly reconstructed myself. I needed money to accomplish this, so I started Nezoi Pharmaceuticals to fund my projects. I made Scando to expand into larger markets. Both functioned as cover-ups for other endeavors."

"But who is Gray?" Death asked again.

"You are Edwin Gray."

What?

DEATH TAKES A PAY CUT

CHAPTER 14

"An old contractor of mine, claiming to be a god, gave me a black substance and asked me to create a new 'Death' for him. Your predecessors kept dying so he wanted one that wouldn't die, or so he told me. I sent out fliers for compensated drug testing, and a thirty-something accountant named Edwin Gray responded first, he took the transformative drug I created, and he became you."

"Are you sure that's right?" Death asked Servos. "Us gods protect and regulate Earth. We aren't made, we exist. The Lord exists."

"I don't know what to tell you," Servos said. "You're Edwin Gray, I made you Death. I have to thank you as well, you paved the way for my research. As a machine, I am not truly alive. With an organic body, I can become real. Edwin, you're living Death. You're proof that I, too, can live. These creatures of soulless flesh were only tests, and now, I have my organic body thanks to you."

Even if what Servos said was true, it didn't explain why Pain would go on a murder spree. Fazed and only growing more confused, Death said nothing.

"You used to live day in, day out wasting your life on numbers. You were so desperate as to sell your soul for cash. Don't you appreciate your new life, your power? Freedom from paperwork?"

"I don't think popping pills equates to selling my soul. It's hard to believe just one made me into Death."

A blip played from Servos' speakers as an envelope appeared on Servos' screen. "Excuse me for a moment," he said. After some seconds, he continued, "Your feelings are shared. Whatever that god of yours gave me was unreal, alien even. Unfortunately, I won't be able to learn what it was."

"You're not dissecting me," Death said.

"That's not why I say such. Rather, I've just been paid an unreal amount to kill you by the same contractor that had me make you. How sad."

"Good, I was starting to hope I'd get the chance to shut you down."

The pod in front of them began to whir. If Death was once this Edwin Gray, what about the rest of the gods? Were any others manufactured? Was The God manufactured? Was The Underworld? Were the heavens? Was anything real? At that moment, the realest thing to Death was ending Servos.

Servos stepped out of the pod, his body coated in bone plating. One metal eye protruded from the center of his head.

"I've hardened this body perfectly. Acid resistant, cut resistant, faultless. Even the glass of this eye could survive a bombing. I am real, I will live my life. What will you do?"

"Like I said, I'm ending you."

Servos clicked his heels, mechanical wheels popping out. The flesh and bone of Servos' arms twisted into blades as he swung for Death. He blocked with the bone on his arms, but he was left with deep cuts.

So he ran.

Death started smashing the cell windows around him. One by one, every kind of horror emerged. To them, Death was rotten meat but Servos had more than enough bone for a chew toy. Death stopped running.

This was his chance. Death looked around and found a storage closet. Inside were shelves with supplies and cans of gasoline, brooms stacked against the wall, and pipes of various kinds that routed through the room. Not much later, he ran back out pouring a trail of gasoline.

"Burning me won't work!" Servos said as he fended off the creatures.

"Just wait a second." Death pressed his elbow against the ground, chalking a circle with the bone. Various symbols were added until a full ritual circle was made. Servos broke through the creatures, speeding towards him. His eye might be bomb-proof, but not his skin. He lit the trail of gasoline leading to the gas main in the storage closet.

Death struck the bone of his knuckles on the ground a few times. Soon enough, he got a spark, igniting the trail. Death pressed his hand to the circle.

"You're too slow." Servos grabbed his arm. White filled their vision.

CHAPTER 15

Through the blurriness and ringing, Death could make out one shape. A yellow face staring back at him. They pushed him backward, waking him. Rubble was everywhere and he couldn't find Servos. It was too dark to see his own hands.

But then, a blue flame appeared. A second, and a third, and more came until he could see. Familiar halls stretched outwards, but they had eroded with age. As he stood up, the flames followed. Whose were they?

Fingers gripped his neck. Death was lifted and flung down one hallway. Behind him was Servos, his mechanical eye broken. "I'd thank you, but this arrangement is less than desirable." He said. "Not even my radio works. However, I am finally alive. One good turn deserves another."

Servos crept closer, falling against the wall every few steps. The pink muscle of his arm snapped and rethreaded itself, stretching towards Death. Death ran as Servos gave chase. Around the corner and deeper into dark corridors, he continued to run. Servos was able to detach his broken wheels, although he continued to stumble.

Winging a left, Death stood against the far wall.

"Are you hiding?" Servos asked. He was blind without his eye, swinging wildly.

Death ducked as the walls crumbled and shook, but Servos grabbed him from the near wall. In one motion, he threw Death into the ceiling as the blue flames were left behind. The protective bone on his back cracked against it before he fell. Servos kicked him before he could get up.

"I know how you feel," Servos said. "To have something taken that you never knew you had. Though you may have been human, you still live. You are not Death, you can be killed, but time won't take its toll. Mortality is a weakness, you shed yours," He kicked him again. "Yet I hadn't begun to live," Again. "To be real." And again. "To be worth something. Believe me, Scando is far from an achievement. Furniture assembly?" He picked up and slammed Death to the floor. "Meatballs?" Slammed again. "As if. You owe me your gift, your undead life, so I have the right to take it." Death tried grabbing at him, but Servos stepped on his arm. Servos choked him until he broke his neck.

But Death got back up. Servos snapped it again, met with the same result.

"You have erased untold numbers of people from Earth, as have I committed scientific atrocities to reach this point. With this last bit of funding, I will live as you have; I will be free. Are you too much of a hypocrite to admit that we are similar in nature?"

"Damn straight." He shot Servos with a shotgun, Servos fell on his backside. The face of Death was no longer his, it was Deceit's. The magic of the Deceit's flames had concealed Death's movements. Shedding the disguise, Deceit stood. The golden rings snapped as a grotesque face burst from the neck, engulfed in blue fire. "Whoever you are, I got the gist of things. You did all of this to be a real boy?"

"I did this to live, I'm doing it to live," Servos said, picking himself up. "Whoever you are, I doubt you're much better than him or me. If either of you think killing me is repentance, you're far from it."

"Not at all, it's just a personal matter."

"Be glad it's not a superiority complex that drives you," Servos said. He swung around the room, missing Deceit. "Not one of you or your gods is the hero of this story," Servos swung again and missed again.

"Over here," Deceit said. His voice echoed from everywhere as the hallways were bright with blue embers.

"Earth is a planet of individuals; nobody is more important than another, so that should include me!"

Death and Deceit ran while Servos was distracted.

"Neat trick." Death said.

"It wasn't one," Deceit said. "These halls just have good acoustics."

"How long were you listening?"

"I'd be grinning ear to ear if we weren't running from that freak."

"Yeah?" Death said.

"After this, we have to celebrate. I never would have expected The Big Guy to be a fraud."

"We don't know that, yet."

"That, or he's weak. Either way, it's a," A claw shot towards them as Deceit pulled Death away. "Win in my book." They kept turning corners, hoping to find an exit. Deceit could teleport anytime with his blessing, but he would be leaving Death behind. Mirages and decoys wouldn't work against Servos, still blind. He asked Death if he could summon anyone. Lucille, Hadad, or even his steed, Drake. The explosion knocked the wind out of Death; incantations nor rituals would work.

"Perfect." Servos had caught up to them. His flailing figure had smoothed itself, shells of bone marbling him whole. An organic eye stretched across his face, all too familiar. "You have your gifts, but I have spent years pivoting from you."

"Save it for Science Weekly; I don't care." Death said.

"I'm faster, stronger, and more durable than you. If you give up, I'll leave you alone."

"So you can kill him?" Deceit asked. "No."

"So I can live! I've said that so many times now, I thought you'd understand by now. Also to kill him."

"What about our revenge?" Deceit turned to Death. "You do want revenge, right?"

"With so much going on, I need a second man." Death was looking worse for wear. "Was I an accountant? That explains a bit."

"Is he okay?" Servos asked. "We can continue this another time."

"What?" Deceit said. "No, no we are not. I didn't come down here to drag him around and take five."

"I could finish my organic body, you both could do what you need before I kill him, win-win."

"My schedule is open, what with my brands blown to bits. We're all immortal, right?"

"He has better things to do than to wait. Don't you, Death?"

"Should I?"

"The god killer, an existential crisis yet to be, a mile of rubble to dig out from?"

From then on, Death could only mumble his words. He wasn't losing blood, but whatever adrenaline a corpse could have had left him. As awkward and inconvenient as it was, the two conscious decided to put murder on hold.

The halls resonated with every scoot as they sat down. Silence echoed, making that indescribable sound of nothing. Eventually, Servos said, "If I may, who are you?"

"You're asking me that now?" Deceit said.

"Yeah."

"Why would I tell you?"

"You shot me."

"You tried to shoot him."

"He tried to kill me."

"You killed him."

"Technically, I didn't."

"Technically, you can shut up."

"And you are?"

"Not listening to you, that's what."

Servos picked up some small rubble, tossing it against the wall across from them. It made a small crater. He picked up another, looked at the wall for a bit, and threw it again. It made a hole that time.

"Want to know how I did it?" Servos asked.

"Did what?"

"Made him."

"Fine."

"Condensing. The root of every solution was condensing. In simple terms, the stuff that turned his skin pitch can squeeze atoms together, meaning he can fit a lot more of them in himself. His atoms are touching, which shouldn't be possible."

"Is that bad?"

"I don't know. That black substance had a lot of impossible properties."

Deceit looked over towards Death. He was out cold lying against the wall. Deceit had thought he looked unsettling before, but his eye was closed. His face appeared as a featureless slab of skin without it.

An hour passed. Servos had thrown a rock hard enough to collapse the adjacent wall, waking Death. He saw Deceit, then the halls' darkness, then Servos.

Deceit asked if Death would start a ritual circle but Death said no. Servos would want to come with them if they tried to leave. Only Death knew how to make them, having learned how years ago when he should have been filing paperwork.

"What are you two chattering about?" Servos asked.

"Leaving." Death said.

"Can I come?"

"No, why would we let you?"

"To kill you sooner?"

"Quit while you're ahead," Deceit said. "Say, if Death was a human, how old was he when Edwin died?"

"Thirty-two."

"Forty-four now, I guess." Death said. "I don't feel forty."

"You'd look two hundred if it weren't for what you're wearing," Deceit said.

"Oh yeah," Death tugged at his uniform, the blue and yellow stripes caked with dust. "I forgot I was wearing this."

The hall went silent for some time, Deceit breaking it, "So, should we get back to the chasing thing?"

"I am amazed by your idiocy," Servos said. "I said you could leave for now."

"You would want to come with us." Deceit turned to Death again. "You still want him dead, right?"

"I guess." Death said

"And we want you dead."

"Am I supposed to care?" Servos asked. "Is that my fault?"

"Everything is your fault! All of this is because of you!"

"Blame your god and blame your ignorance, but don't blame me. You, Edwin, were enough of a fool to take that pill blindly. I fulfilled a contract; my ulterior motives had no bearing on it."

"That isn't my problem, and it isn't his either."
"Whose problem?"

Death pointed to Servos' left. A skeletal horse rushed towards him, trampling past as Death and Deceit climbed on. Servos yelled something at them but neither of them could hear over the horse's, Drake's, gallop. Death told Drake that they needed the quickest way up to the surface, so off he went.

Servos sped towards them in a full sprint. He was getting used to working a physical body, simulations could only go so far, but he couldn't catch up to them.

CHAPTER 16

It was late morning now. The sun hung above a pleasant New Wattsonville. Death stood atop Scando's roof, far from Nezoi Pharmaceuticals. He still had Pain to deal with. Maybe Pain was right, but why would they be? He wasn't sure what to believe now. Even so, he wouldn't believe in a murder spree.

Death chanted words he hadn't in so many years, "Heavens, may thy grace carry my soul to your domain. May I walk all that blankets the Earth." An invisible force carried Death upwards into The Lord's realm. His head poked through the clouds. He expected to see angels or gods going about their days. Angelic bodies paved the way to The Almighty's halls. Virtues, Powers, even Seraphim lied motionless. Pain had arrived first.

He walked slowly as if to pay respects despite his loathing. Up stairs of fine marble, he found the bodies of gods. Narcotics, Cobbling, and even big shots like

Fate and Love bled gold. And finally, there Pain was, waiting for Death. He was facing the gates to the throne room, although far removed from the throne itself. They turned with their three eyes boring into Death's one.

"Well?" Death asked. "I went there. I am not me. Do you feel like explaining yourself now?"

"None of us were ever supposed to exist. We were all made by The False God, except for you."

"Do the other gods know?"

"They know you were made, believing they are the only ones pure."

"What about The Lord? Why did he do it?"

"Not long ago, I learned he was made too. Remember last year's gala?"

"Yeah, I got a gift basket of bread from it. Just bread."

"Well anyhow, I was guarding The False God's throne as he gave speeches in heaven's halls. Out of lone curiosity, I wandered into his private room and saw his source of power. It felt identical to him, the white meteorite supplying his power."

"So a magic rock made him a god?"

"It's not that far of a leap. I interrogated some of his closest gods, and I learned the truth. We were all humans centuries ago. You, however, left the world as Edwin Gray in 2012."

All of it was a lie. The heavens, The Underworld, and the gods themselves. Death said, "So what? Is this supposed to be justice? Killing that faker?"

"I'm balancing the world. We were never meant to exist; we were never meant to control Earth."

"Then break the stone! Make him powerless."

"He has lived his life, as have I. You are still young and deserving of your life. However, you have the strength to slay The False God. For Earth to live, to truly be free, you must die to serve as my tool, Edwin. I will shape you into my strongest weapon against him."

"Even if I could be, even if he's lived long enough, what about the other gods? Do they deserve to die?"

"No god is a gift and no evil is made apart by the divine, even if they believe so. We do not serve as the mirror to man, they are the lens through which we are focused. If purpose is what you seek, I shall grant it. Come, abandon yourself, and we will break the chains forthright."

Death walked up to Pain as Pain held out their hand. He took their hand with a firm shake; he pulled them close and plunged his other fist into Pain "I like myself, thank you." It went deep into them, almost through them.

"I see. You are more than I anticipated."

"Oh." Death was genuinely sorry. "I thought you were stronger? I mean, you were stronger before.

"You are Death, aren't you? Cold, inescapable, inevitable?"

"You knew I could kill you? Why do any of this then? Was this all just a suicide mission?"

One of Pain's eyes turned to dust. "I didn't. I needed the most violent gods gone before I could attack. I didn't foresee you gaining such strength, nor such from an unknown source. Also, I had thought you would be too shocked by your true identity to go against me." Pain's eyes started to flicker. "Please, end the false god. Won't you?" Death dislodged his fist from Pain as they crumbled into nothing. Death removed his Scando uniform, it felt wrong now. He felt better wearing his suit and tie.

Through the gates of the heavens, under golden braziers, past more and more corpses, Death reached the throne. There he sat, The Mightiest God.

"You came." Said he.

"You didn't give me much of a choice, bounty and all." He said.

"Am I next? Was Pain a stepping stone to me?"

"Are you going to put up a fight?"

"I don't fight. I am truth and I am pure." Life was gone. The other gods were busy. Angels stained the clouds gold. "I know what you think of him, but cast those thoughts away. He has left me here, alone and defenseless."

"The gods won't follow a martyr. I spent twelve years thinking you were divine. Although I disliked you, I don't know how to feel. Down in The Underworld, I was myself. As Death or as Edwin, it doesn't matter. The others believe they are gods, that they share the holiness you were said to be. I used to be someone, so I wonder what they'll think of your shiny rock; how they owe themselves to coincidence."

"A coincidence they won't find. See for yourself." The god opened his arm towards the room behind him, inviting.

Death walked past, eyeing the god. Inside that back room was a bed thrice his size. A balcony opened towards the heavens' plains, lush for sheep to graze. Only the light shining in illuminated the room, for only the heavens' light is pure. The god's scriptures hung on the other wall, stored for banquet speeches or meetings. Laid on an altar in the room's center, a red pillow beneath, the meteor shone dull.

It didn't glow and it didn't shimmer, although crystalline. If anything, it looked like a geode from a cheap gift shop. It was familiar. Despite his amnesia, Death was sure he hadn't seen it before. Poking it, rubbing it, and putting his ear up to it did nothing. The meteor didn't feel like the god; what Pain had described was gone.

"Are you sure this thing works?" Death called back.

"It works," said he. "However, I decided to use it another way. I'm sure you've heard of your replacement, yes? It's about time you meet them."

From nowhere, a helmeted man appeared. A bullet pierced Death's skull.

CHAPTER 17

Death was dead. Blackness filled his vision. He hung in the end of his life. Whatever he was, he wasn't a ghost and he wasn't a soul of The Underworld. Across from him, wherever this was, stood someone wearing a yellow mask.

"Wow, what a twist!" They said. "Death dying, huh? I have got to hand it to them, this one isn't that bad."

"Sorry, who are you? I'm supposed to be dying right now." He said.

"You're well past that. Life? Death? You won't be finding either of those here."

He tried feeling around, his limbs weighed by whatever he was submerged in. It wasn't water, so how could he see?

"As much as I'd like to help," They said. "There's not much I can do. Y'know, greater powers and all that."

"Who are you?"

"Although, the first time I was here, I was stuck for a century or two before I escaped."

Death couldn't feel his skin. It felt cold. "You were stuck here before? How did you get out?"

"Effort and time, lots of both. Also, sorry about that boss of yours."

"Boss? You know Servos?"

"Servos? Man, I almost forgot about him. No, I mean the glowy one. I ought to get zippered pockets after that debacle."

"Can you stop changing the topic?"

"It should have happened already, why hasn't it?" the person said to themselves. They looked troubled. Two white dots peered from the mask's eyeholes. "Alright, look: I'm not supposed to do this, but I don't think your human spirit's going to figure it out any time soon. Bill Crocker, that's the guy you have to kill."

"I have to kill someone named Bill to leave here? Is that what you did? Where even is 'here?'"

"No, no. Well, yes, but that's not what I did. I don't know how you should kill him. Perhaps your scythe? Wait, you don't have that this time around. Strangulation? His own gun? You're Death, it's not my job to figure out how. That is, if you want to be Death still."

Who else would he be? Edwin? It was too late for that.

"Who am I kidding?" They said, "There's no real choice. Just do your thing and you'll be fine."

"Why am I not on Earth?"

"Half of you isn't from Earth– and I'm not talking about that crystal I dropped. Honestly, no part of you is anymore. So, shut up and off Crocker already! See you then." The person disappeared, leaving him there.

Bill Crocker. That was a human name. He should be dead according to memory. At that point, however, there wasn't a 'should be.' It was only what the god had wanted.

Death reached outwards. His arm wasn't rotting, it was matte. The bones were gone. So were his fingernails. He was only the shape of a person. With the shape of his hand, he grasped something: the neck of Bill Crocker.

CHAPTER 18

The visor of Crocker's motorcycle helmet reflected Death's face. It was sleek and angular like plastic. Behind Crocker was the god, his featurelessness emanating shock.

"This is your replacement?" Death asked. "Some guy you plucked off the street?"

"You should be dead." Said he.

"I should be Edwin, but look where we are." Death snapped Crocker's neck with his hand. Crocker's head flopped, but it soon stood back up.

"My mistake was entrusting power to a machine, but never again. Most of the meteor is within this man now."

"So you made him immortal and gave him a gun?"

"No, I made someone I can control. I am the meteor, the meteor is me, and so is he."

Crocker raised his handgun, Death bashing it. The grip didn't loosen. Snapping his neck didn't work again. Unable to do much else, Death pushed him down into the clouds; down into Earth.

"You really should have made him an angel." Death said. "There goes your immortal."

Crocker burst from the clouds, carried by crystalline wings glowing as bright as the god. The same crystals had grown around his neck. Unexpectedly, he wasn't alone. The other gods started emerging from beneath the clouds. The Underworld's forces weren't strong enough. Abundance was the first, multiplying Crocker's gun-toting arms tenfold. Size made him larger, Growth turned the crystals into armor, and Rallying brought more gods.

Gods piled in by the hundreds, all adding something. Crocker soon became a monstrosity, towering over the heavens. Limbs human, mechanical, and animal sprouted from him as crystals rooted in the ground from his legs. Golden bile seeped from his pores as the heavens itself joined his mass. Death was no longer standing on clouds, he was standing on this abomination.

The god was nowhere to be seen. He had given all he had to Crocker; to this stranger. Bill Crocker's life had ended to serve him. Finally, the god appeared beside Death.

"My final work." Said he. "The cornerstone of humanity's preservation: Yggdrasil. Does it not amaze you?"

"Can't you name it something original?" Death tried to keep his balance.

"Let's see... How about, The World Tree?"

"How about Crocker? That's who it is. Crocker."

By that point, Crocker had grown to the size of a skyscraper. Foreign limbs hung like branches, crystals holding each in place.

"Have it your way." Said he. With the motion of the god's hand, Crocker swung its branches at Death.

He hit one of Crocker's disfigured arms, but the crystals filled the bruise. They were too large to make a dent in and too resilient to permanently harm. Another swing and kick did nothing.

"What is Crocker meant for anyways?" Death shouted.

"I have become too old for my divine responsibility. This tree shall govern The Heavens and the underworld."

"All you ever did was sit on that throne and tell us gods what to do! You made us take your responsibilities."

"Yes, I won't be needing any of you either." The other gods were nearby, but they were confused. One by one, each of them dropped from the clouds. "As much as it pains me to say this, Pain was right. These thoughts and opinions muck up The Heavens; Earth requires universal order."

Death watched as each god fell to their death. He hoped Deceit had stayed back on Earth's surface. "Why?" He asked. "Why control Earth to begin with?"

"I am tens of centuries old. I have seen the rise and fall of every great civilization; I have seen mankind's lapses and their accomplishments. Only I can preserve Earth best."

"Who said that was your decision to make?"

"I myself, the highest authority. Although, you may answer to this Crocker. He serves well as my second in command."

At that moment, Crocker flung Death off itself. He plummeted. With some quick incantations, Lucille emerged from a rift.

"You have wings, Lucille?" Death asked.

"Whatever you desire, Mr. Reaper."

Lucille set him down atop Scando. "What is that in the sky?" She asked.

"That's Crocker. All you need to know is that it's bad."

DEATH TAKES A PAY CUT

Crocker loomed above New Wattsonville. Its crystal roots had wrapped around the heavens as if they were nothing more than soil. The trunk consisted of odd patches of flesh and scales and unfamiliar mass. Some branches were limbs and some were disfigurements of nature. It was taller.

"Do you have a plan?" Lucille asked Death.

"No. If I hit it, it hardens with crystals. I can't break the crystals and it's too high up for me to try anyway."

"I could help, Mr. Reaper," Lucille said.

"But then what? I keep swinging?"

"Sure," she said. "What's worse?"

"Dying. Again. Probably for the third time."

There wasn't time for a plan. High above, Crocker writhed as New Wattsonville was awash with light. The Earth shook violently. Crystal roots burst from the fallen gods' corpses, holy statues burst from the ground, and Scando rose. The roof beneath cracked and gave way. Falling fast, Death could only say, "Lucille, protect The Underworld if you can!"

He hit the ground, cracking the white flowcrete beneath him. No bones broken. No bones. There wasn't any sensation. He could hear and see, but no smell, touch, or taste. He missed saliva.

The white hall extended before him, arrows projected from spotlights onto the floor. Forwards was forever and so was back, but the shelves had holes in them. Death tried pushing a shelf to the side, but the whole of it turned black and was sucked into his skin.

He had no skin. Either that or the shelf turned into more of his skin. Through the shelf's absence was a four-story cylinder of escalators. It was like Sears, but it had the smooth laminate and Scandinavian simplicity of Scando. Across from him, pasted on the wall, was Scando's instruction booklet mascot wearing a black vest, custodian helmet, and holding a baton.

"Growing pains were bound to come," The god said, appearing before Death with a burst of light. "But greatness comes with struggle."

"You scared the Hell out of me!" Death said. "Why are you here?"

"I was afraid something like this might happen. Your presence warps my grand design. This was to be a great colosseum showcasing man's achievement! Instead, you have given me this."

"If that's the case, blame Crocker. No, blame yourself. You decided to make a world-shaping tree without knowing what would happen."

"It is yet to be world-shaping, though that is my goal. Once Yggdrasil–"

"–Crocker."

"Once The World Tree settles its roots into Wattsonland, it shall uplift the Earth by its core!"

"It's New Wattsonville."

"Wattsonland was America's sole antediluvian and medieval kingdom until 1852. Succumbing to modern government, it continued as Wattsonville until 1947," As the god said this, Death started climbing the escalator. "At which point two fools dressed as medieval knights used pyrotechnics to burn it all down. Thus, New Wattsonville came after."

"Then why did you get it wrong?"

"I am everywhere. I am the light that casts every shadow, I am day against night," His speech went on as Death navigated the twisting halls of Scando Mall. Preaching seemed to be the god's only skill.

As Death walked further into the labyrinth, he started to notice storefronts. Women's clothes, soft pretzels, and cheap fidget toys all in cold lighting. Decorative plants and staircases and more soon sprouted. If The God was correct, that Death's presence warped the space around him, why was it turning into a mall? None of it was familiar.

One store out of the many caught his eye, brightly lit. It was a self-serve candy store with pistachio walls and white trimmings. Inside, he found jelly beans and black licorice and chocolate-coated crickets kept separate on a shelf. There was a back door to the right of the register, but it was fuzzy. Every time Death looked at it, turning his head away and back a few times, he couldn't process it.

Soon, something emerged from the door; through the wood of the door. It kept moving, and melting, and it was hard to look at like a bright lightbulb. There was one distinct feature: a vertical, cyclopean eye filling its face.

"Hey, mightiest fraud!" Death called out. "What is that and why does it have Servos' eye?"

Death started backing away as The God appeared to say, "What is what? I'm not seeing it."

"What happened to that all-seeing," Death stumbled backwards into some jars of caramels. The glass shattered, the shards soaking into his arm. He groaned and stood back up. "Eye, I meant eye."

"I see, you have finally succumbed to the insanity of your wretched existence."

The mass of light slid across the counter, crushing it with its weight. The room felt cold, and the counter was sucked into the creature. As Death tried to summon his back away, the thing turned black as its eye paled to white. In the blink of an eye, a jaw emerged from the mass to snap. Death's arm melted and swirled involuntarily, shaping into a blade. It stabbed through and the teeth clamped around it, sacrificed to make the killing strike.

It didn't hurt. He couldn't feel any of his arm, or himself. He felt cold. The creature, however, started to lose its shape. It looked around in panic, spikes protruding and melting and stabbing again. All of it shrunk, the eye included, into Death's lost arm.

His arm wriggled on the tile floor, no; he wriggled his arm. Picking it up, Death reattached it.

"I am Death." said Death.

"That was your designation," The God said. "But what is your point in saying such?"

"I mean it. I can't die. Didn't you see," before death could finish his sentence, he suddenly found himself sucked into black nothingness again. It was colder than before, and the figure with the yellow mask was closer.

"No, he didn't." The figure said. "You can blame me for that. We could only see it since it's also us, and so is the rest of that mall."

"What are we? Why am I here again?"

"I wish I could explain, but we don't have the time."

"Why not? You brought me here again, there is nothing around, what is stopping you?"

"Many things, or one thing. I hate being cryptic about everything, but it's what I'm forced to do. I think that's what they're telling me to do."

"Who's telling you?"

"Nobody that I know, I just know they're there and I have to comply. I know what they are though."

"You're complicated, everything is. Every time I reach the end there's another face waiting. Servos, The God, Crocker, you, and here."

"You're right. I'm supposed to tell you to soldier on, that more of those creatures are coming and you must kill them. You're supposed to wander these halls encountering strange sights and warped memories before escaping, met by the thankful smiles of those you've had such little time to meet. Then, newfound strength and pride carry you to the heavens again to cut down that tree. The day will be saved, you will be successful, and life will return to the way it was for a time. You might not reach your supposed end; you won't reach me. However, you stand here knowing of something bigger. Is that correct?"

Death looked into the figure's eyes. They were deep and shallow; they were as self-contradicting as they were still; they had multitudes. If Death was this figure, and they were him, however that may be. They must feel the same despite their differences.

He took a breath, in whatever way he could without lungs, and said to the figure, "Things may end, I might win, but will there still be obstacles afterwards"

"It depends," The figure said. "I can't say for certain because I'm told not to. It's all very vague and confusing and dissatisfying if you ask me."

"Dissatisfying to you?"

"Sure, but I may not be alone in that feeling."

Death sat down. There was nothing to sit on, but he figured with all of the confusion and strangeness that the lack of a chair didn't matter. It wasn't that nothing mattered, he hadn't become a nihilist because some stranger spoke strangely. Sitting down mattered, and so he sat on the void they were inside.

"So what now?" Death asked. "If all you say is true, that those events should come to pass, there's no telling what will happen now that I know. If you're lying or mistaken, would there be any consequences for not listening?" The figure stared at him, sure of what to say but hesitant to say it. Death continued, "I've come to understand that you can't say or that you may not know the answer yourself. It won't be any less random if you do or don't. I've seen gods, robots, and even aliens. That was what you were implying earlier, right? That half of myself isn't from Earth."

"Does it matter? From space or not, it's alien to you."

"It defies the laws of everything I know."

"Indeed. I've changed my mind, or perhaps

they have. It's hard to tell if my decisions are my own," The figure straightened their back. Their eyes were focused for the first time. "You choose what to do. Fight those who oppose you and restore peace; Search for any way possible to take back the human life that was taken from you; Give yourself to the meaningless of choice and live only for the whims of life. Whatever you pick, you must move forward. Into victory, into safety, or into uncertainty."

"I will move forward. I have to put an end to everything if I am to say hello or goodbye, don't I?"

"For most there is an end. The end gives meaning to the beginning. You aren't most, there isn't necessarily an end for you."

"Maybe. I guess I'll see."

"I am eager to see what you choose. They aren't for some reason, but they're calm."

Death stood up. As he did, the void retreated to the nowhere it came from. It took the figure with it, or perhaps the figure took the void. Looking down at his arm, Death could feel the mass of the creature's corpse within. He didn't feel that he had grown or that he was stuffed with it; he felt denser.

"What was that?" The God asked.

"Did you see that?" Death asked.

"Yes, your eye flickered like a lightbulb."

"Oh," Death thought for a moment. "I was just blinking."

"You blink? I was wondering whether it would shut vertically or horizontally. It is rather tall and sharp."

"Sure."

Whoever the figure was, whoever the aforementioned "they" was, it seemed that there would always be another conflict. Where did the figure come from and what connected Death to them? If he found the answer, he would want to know the origins of the figure, the cause of those origins, and so on. It was endless.

Despite it all, despite the self-fulfilling prophecy, Death pressed on. He escaped the labyrinth of unfamiliar memories, he laid Crocker to rest, he went home, and he sat at his desk. He heard the click of heels across the black marble floor.

"Hello Mr. Reaper, ready for another day?"

Made in the USA
Middletown, DE
06 August 2024